The Miss Hobbema Pageant

W.P. KINSELLA

The Miss Hobbema Pageant

HarperPerennial
HarperCollins*Publishers*Ltd

ACKNOWLEDGMENTS

The following stories have previously appeared in print:
"Being Invisible" in *Western Living*, and as part of a Southam Press series on literacy, it appeared in the *Sunday Toronto Star*, the *Vancouver Sun* and several other newspapers; "Snitches" in *Queen's Quarterly*; "Pizza Ria" in *Edmonton Magazine* and *Vancouver Magazine*; "The Sundog Society" in *Wisconsin Review*; "The Election" in *Whetstone*; "Graves" in *Canadian Forum*; "Homer" in *Matrix*; "A Hundred Dollars Worth of Roses" in *New Quarterly*. Both "Homer" and "A Hundred Dollars Worth of Roses" were published in the chapbook *Five Stories* (Vancouver: Hoffer/TANKS, 1986).

THE MISS HOBBEMA PAGEANT

First published by HarperCollins Publishers Ltd: 1989
First HarperPerennial edition: 1995

Canadian Cataloguing in Publication Data

Kinsella, W. P.
The Miss Hobbema pageant

"1st HarperPerennial ed."
ISBN 0-00-647960-X

I. Title.

PS8571.I57M58   C813'.54   C89-094845-3
PR9199.3.K55M58

---

95 96 97 98 99 ❖ HC 10 9 8 7 6 5 4 3 2 1

Printed and bound in the United States

For my daughter
Shannon Leah Kinsella

Contents

The Miss Hobbema Pageant

Being Invisible

The only time my friend Frank Fencepost ever raise up his fist to me was four or five years ago, when I suggest that maybe he should learn to read and write.

Frank and me been friends since before either of us can remember. When we was babies my mom and his used to put us in the same apple box, tie a string to it, slide us down the long hill to Blue Quills Hall or Hobbema General Store.

"You used to look like a couple of caterpillars in your snowsuits," Ma say to me once. "Even back then Frank could cry louder than any kid on the reserve."

I been covering for Frank, all through Grade School, and at the Tech School in Wetaskiwin where we studying to be mechanics. But I don't mind 'cause I'm not much of a fighter, even though I'm bigger and taller than Frank. And Frank be ready to mix it up as soon as he make eye contact with somebody, and he's mean as a bagful of bobcats when he get riled.

People think it's odd that me and Frank are friends, because we are about as opposite as two guys can be. There ain't no place Frank is afraid to go and almost nothing he is afraid to do.

Frank he run on instinct, while I think way too much. I wish I was as outgoing as Frank and that I could speak up smart answers the way he does. I mean after there been a run in with Chief Tom and Pastor Orkin, I always think of something smart I could of said, a week or two after it happen. And I'd like to take some really crazy chances sometimes, the way Frank do, and I'd like to be able to stare a white girl in the eye until she make friends with me. Frank, though he hardly ever let on, is proud of me because of all the stories I got printed up.

I guess that's why we like each other; we each got something about him that the other one don't.

"I ain't *ever* goin' to," he say, and shake his fist under my nose.

"I just suggest it as a friend," I say. "It's not like you ain't smart. If you put half as much effort into learning to read as you do hiding the fact you can't, you'd be able to out read and out write me."

"According to a magazine I read," I go on, "there's over four million people in Canada who can't read enough to get by. So you ain't alone."

"Four million," say Frank. "That would fill up Blue Quills Hall a couple of times I bet. Maybe even as many people as came to the Duran Duran concert in Edmonton."

"At least that many," I say, glad Frank ain't thinking about punching my face anymore.

We walking down the main street of Wetaskiwin, heading towards the Alice Hotel where we supposed to meet our girl-friends, when Frank ask me to read the lettering on the side of a bright-painted van. That was how come I suggested he should learn himself to read.

"You know, Frank," I said, "there ain't nothing wrong with admitting you can't do something."

"Yeah, but I'm supposed to know how."

"Who's the toughest guy on the reserve?" I ask, look like I'm changing the subject.

"Me."

"Come on. Who would you least like to have mad at you, and know they was going to pound you good the next time they seen you?"

"Mad Etta."

"Seriously."

"I am serious," and Frank dance backwards down the street. "Well, maybe Robert Coyote."

Robert's fists is hard as if he holding a brick in each one, and he is the meanest street-fighter for I bet a hundred miles.

"You know Robert never learned to read until the last time he was in jail. He wasn't afraid to admit he couldn't."

"Yeah, but he's so tough he could wear panties and a bra to the Alice Hotel bar and nobody would laugh at him."

"Still he admitted he couldn't read, and they taught him down at Drumheller Jail."

I remember Robert joking about it when he got back to town. First thing he did was read all the signs behind the counter at Hobbema Pool Hall: NO CREDIT, NO FOUL LANGUAGE.

Robert laugh when he read that last sign, and he blast off enough swear words to turn Pastor Orkin green.

"You going to write down stories like Silas now that you learned how?" somebody ask him.

"Nah, I ain't gonna write nothing but bad checks," and he grin wicked. "The reason I let them teach me was all the guys in the joint got dirty books in their cells. And I couldn't read them. I had to be stuck with looking at the pictures in *Hustler* and *Penthouse*. They sent this woman down from Calgary to teach us and I signed up. She started us with little kids' picture books with about one word to a page.

"About the second class I bring in one of these dirty books. 'This here's what I want to learn to read from,' is what I say. She look at the title. '*Call Girls in Bondage*,' she read out loud, and the other guys in the class all laugh. 'I think you'll have to wait three or four classes before you can read this,' she say, but she smile at me real nice and I can tell she's there for more than just teaching reading and writing. There's a lot of women who get off on being around dangerous men, and she was one of them.

"I think it was the sixth week, I stay after class with my little book again. I can read most of it by then, and I pick out a real sexy part, say I'm having trouble with the words.

"She's never supposed to be alone with one of us guys. But I ain't surprised when she close the door to her office. I was sure sorry that class only last twelve weeks, and so was she."

"That your way of telling me I got to go to jail to learn to read?" Frank asked.

"You ought to do it," Robert say. "It couldn't make you any dumber than you are now, Fencepost," and he punch Frank's arm, leave bruises for about a month. But even Robert saying it okay to learn don't convince Frank.

But it look to me like he's weakening. I keep *reading* and *writing* in the conversation at the bar and at the Gold Nugget Café afterward. At the café, Frank he study the menu with a fierce eye, then he order for all four of us. I bet I only read that menu to Frank twice, and that was years ago, but he memorized the whole thing—something I couldn't do.

"Come on, Frank, why don't you give it a try?" says his girl, Connie.

"Will you teach me, Silas?"

"I suppose I could try to teach you, but I don't know the methods, and I don't think I should."

"I ain't goin' to school with no babies."

"You won't have to. Up in Edmonton, at Grant MacEwan Community College, they have what are called Adult Literacy classes. I read about them in the newspaper."

"Seems like a funny place for them to advertise for people who can't read," says Frank.

"You know, Silas," says Connie, "one time I told Frank he wasn't gonna get any more lovin' from me until he learned to write *I Love You Connie Bigcharles*. But you know Frank . . . ," and she break into a sweet smile and hug Frank's neck.

"One hug is worth a thousand words," says Frank.

Late that night, while me and Frank are sitting at his cabin, Frank says, "You know what I'd like more than anything else? To be able to read your books. I don't know how else to say it, Silas, but when you can't read or write, it kind of like being invisible."

"I never thought of it like that."

"It's like having a bad scar in a place nobody can see, or a disease on the inside of you."

"They can cure diseases," I say, "especially ones like yours that ain't fatal. You *could* be like James Redbird who got the multiple sclerosis. Ain't nothing can be done for that."

"Yeah," says Frank. "Hey, remember that dumb job I had?"

One summer Frank he got work at the John Deere Tractor Store in Wetaskiwin. It wasn't fixing tractors like we been trained to do. He got to swamp out the garage and be a general gofer. Frank did a good job, and in a couple of weeks when the assistant in the parts department went on holidays they decided to move Frank to the order desk, where he would have had to fill out forms and read work sheets. Frank, who usually afraid of nothing, quit the job altogether, rather than admit he couldn't read.

"I remember," I say.

"I don't usually quit things. I just wasn't brave enough to let them know about my trouble."

"It isn't a question of being brave. It's just a matter of wanting a little more out of life."

"Yeah, but neither of my folks were able to read. A lot of older people get by . . ."

"Times are changing too much. There's no place you can hide any more. You can't go out on a trap line and just stay there. There's no place government forms don't get to these days."

Frank laugh. "You know down at the Tech School, they've never caught on because nobody there believes there's people who can't read and write. I told them in the office one day when they wanted me to fill out some form. 'Hey,' I said, 'I can't read this, and even if I could I can't write enough to fill it out!' 'Stop goofing off, Fencepost,' the office girl say to me. 'If you couldn't read and write you wouldn't be here.' "

"So you brought it to me and I filled it out for you."

"Right. Silas, if I go, you got to come with me."

"You're still a little afraid?"

"Hey, a Fencepost is afraid of nothing."

"It's all right to be afraid. You're going to do something totally new."

"I'm not afraid."

"I know. Here, let me show you something," and I open up one of my books. "Look at these rows and rows of squiggly black lines. You're not afraid of those are you?"

"Of course not."

"You're smarter than any row of squiggles."

"Damn right."

"Well, all you're gonna learn is how to outsmart those little alphabet letters. They got secrets they been keepin' from you. But you're gonna beat them at their own game."

"Right," says Frank. "Still . . ."

"You'd like a little company?"

"Yeah."

"Okay, you got it. But I'm just gonna sit beside you. The teacher ain't gonna want me in the class because I read and write, and because I ain't paid. When she asks what I'm doin' there, you tell her I'm your friend and that I'm mute and need looking after, okay?"

"Okay," says Frank.

The registration take place at the office for Continuing Education.

I read the catalog to Frank.

There is a beginning and an advanced course in basic English for reading-disadvantaged people.

"Hey, none of this beginning stuff for me," says Frank "I got years of experience as an illiterate. I want to go in the advanced class."

I fill out the application to put Frank in the beginning class. We take the form to the counter. The woman there look it over and then say to me, "We'll need some proof of your illiteracy, Mr. Post."

"How about if you ask me to read that sign on the wall and I'll say I can't," says Frank.

"I notice you've signed your application."

"When I was just a kid, Silas here wrote out my name and I learned to copy it down. It don't mean anything, honest."

"Well . . ."

"How many people who can read and write sneak into these literacy classes?" I ask.

The secretary give me a mean look.

But that was about the only bureaucracy we suffer.

Like Frank ask, I go with him to the first class. In the afternoon Frank he bought himself a 100-page notebook with a picture of Blondie, the rock-and-roll singer, on the cover. He also acquired, as five-finger bargains, about a dozen felt pens, the same kind I use to write my stories.

"You figure I should get two pads in case I fill this one up tonight?"

"I think one will be enough for the first class."

The group meet in an ordinary classroom at Grant MacEwan College. The room is too hot and the lights are too bright. There is about 15 people there, all sit shy and stare at their feet. There is a lady about Ma's age, who look Indian, so we sit next to her. There is also a man and woman, look to be Chinese, a dark man wear a red turban, while the rest is white, range from a guy about our age to an old man with a white moustache.

The teacher is young and pretty and introduce herself as Elizabeth

Stranger. She call out everybody's name, and as she do, people raise their hands so she can check them off her list.

"There are three more people here than I have on my list," she says. "Did someone bring a friend along for moral support? That's quite all right, you know."

Frank's hand shoot up.

"My friend here is nude. He need lookin' after."

The teacher smile nice, but puzzled.

"You can't tell by the way he looks. But he can't say a word, even if you was to pay him a dollar."

I'd have had Frank here years ago if I could talk like Miss Stranger. In half an hour she have people feeling good about themselves and so proud they make the move to come to class they can hardly wait to get started.

"I know what you've gone through," Miss Stranger say. "Every billboard, every storefront, every banner is a constant reminder that you can't read. You learn to lie, to invent reasons why you can't read aloud from a book. And you develop an elephant's memory.

"People who are illiterate have to memorize signs, sometimes whole forms or order blanks; you have to guess at the meaning of words from other clues. I remember once I went to apply for a job and I stood outside a door with the word PERSONNEL written on it, studied it for a long time trying to guess what it might be. Finally I asked someone where the Personnel Office was. They pointed at the door and said, "What's the matter, can't you read?""

That was the way she let us know she been illiterate at one time, too.

"Illiteracy has virtually nothing to do with intelligence. You've all become experts in failure, but, starting tonight, we're going to put an end to your failures."

Miss Stranger get out some cards with pictures and letters on them. The letter A got a picture of an apple, the letter B the picture of a bear, and so on.

"You still want me to stay?" I ask Frank at intermission.

Frank is walking along the walls, stopping at each poster or notice he come to, point out to me and anybody else who care to listen, which letters is A's, B's and C's.

"Maybe just to the end of this class. I hope we learn some whole words when we go back in. And, Silas," Frank grin kind of sheepish at me, like he do when he get caught in a lie, "thanks for keeping after me," and he clap my shoulder with his hand.

Second half of the class Miss Stranger ask each person to tell why he or she want to learn to read and write.

"My wife just had a baby," say the guy about my age, "and I want to be able to read bedtime stories to him, like my old man did for me."

"I want to read the Bible," say the Indian woman near us, "and to pass the word of the Lord on to my friends and relatives."

We move a couple of seats farther away so people won't think we're with her.

"I am tired of working on the assembly line," say the man with the turban. "I wish to be employed in the office."

"I want to be able to write bad checks," says Frank when his turn come.

"I see," says Miss Stranger, while most everyone laugh. "Well, Mr. Fencepost, we're an equal-opportunity literacy class. Just don't call on me as a character witness if you get arrested."

"When he gets arrested, not if . . . ," I say.

"I thought you were mute," says Miss Stranger.

"This here's Silas Ermineskin who's had about five books printed up, and I'm gonna learn to read them all," says Frank.

The teacher smile and go on with the lesson.

The first three or four weeks Frank get real frustrated that they don't teach him faster. He bug me about 12 hours a day to help him sound out words and make up alphabet letters.

But then he catch on to reading a few words together, and he learn to write short sentences. One day he come to me with "My brother is a green pig" written on a sheet of paper.

I check the spelling and that all the letters is made right.

"I never knew you could write down things that wasn't possible," Frank say. I have to puzzle over that for a while. Guess only someone who just discover the wonder of writing would think that way.

I pick Frank up when his last class is over. He come out holding a little certificate that says he has satisfactorily completed the Adult Literacy Class. He read the certificate to me about 50 times, point out his name each time. He even read the name of the printer, which is in real tiny letters in the bottom corner.

We park the truck downtown, decide to go have a drink to celebrate.

As we walk, Frank turn in circles, like a dog chasing his tail, afraid he going to miss some of the signs we pass by.

"BUS STOP. NO PARKING," read Frank. "SEASON'S GREETINGS."

He stare all around for something else to read, his head going from side to side as his eyes search.

"PLUMBING AND HEATING," he read from a neon sign

across the street. "GOLD COINS BOUGHT AND SOLD. COMPLETE LINE OF WALLPAPER, PAINT AND STAIN," he call out as we pass store windows.

"HAMBURGERS, FRENCH FRIES, APPLE PIE," he go on. "JOHN THE LOCKSMITH, KEYS CUT. TRAVEL AGENCY. ON SALE. DIAMOND RINGS. MARY LYLE'S BEAUTY SALON."

Then we come to a broad fence have a whole lot of writing on it. There is the peace sign, and below it someone has written NUKE THE WHALES. There are about two dozen four-letter words. And among them is written LOVE IS A FOUR-LETTER WORD. Someone else wrote SAVE THE SALMON, CAN AN INDIAN.

"Hey, Silas," Frank yell, "I always wanted to be able to write on a wall."

I think I know how excited he is. It must be something like the feeling I had the first time I got a letter saying one of my stories was to be printed in a magazine.

I watch as Frank take out a felt pen, study the fence for a while before he write THE GREAT FENCEPOST WAS HERE! Then he smile something fierce and go bounding off down the street.

He get at least a half a block ahead of me. The streets are quiet and there is frost on the parking meters and trolley wires.

"CRAWFORD AND KIRK, ATTORNEYS AT LAW," he is yelling. "CANADA TRUST. TOYOTA COROLLA. PASSENGER LOADING ZONE AT ALL TIMES . . ."

Snitches

E very once in a while my father, Paul Ermineskin, show up here on the reserve. He is long enough between visits that most everyone forget, or forgive, or just push to the back of their mind the rotten things he done the last time he was here.

"Hey, Silas," he say to me, when he come over to my table at the Alice Hotel bar in Wetaskiwin. I seen him sitting in the corner with his old friend Isaac Hide, but I just hoped he wouldn't see me, or if he did that he'd have sense enough to keep to himself. "Long time, son."

"Not long enough," is what I want to say, but instead I take the hand he stick out. His hand is dry as a sweetgrass braid. Pa don't look as bad as he sometimes does. He's had his hair cut recently and is wearing new jeans and a red-and-white checkered mackinaw.

"I see you still got the prettiest girl on the reserve," he say, more to Sadie than to me, and he hug Sadie's shoulder. "Guess likin' pretty girls runs in the family."

"Only I don't get drunk and break their ribs and black their eyes," I'd like to say, but again I stay quiet.

"Nice to see you, Mr. Ermineskin," Sadie says, and hug one arm around his waist. He sure knows how to get around people. Sadie is nice, but she ain't pretty to anyone but me.

"You're gonna pay for that compliment," I'd like to say to her. "He'll probably borrow money from you before the night's over." Instead, when I speak I speak to Pa: "What you up to?" He's still standing and I don't make any move to ask him to sit, though there's an extra chair at the table.

"Me and Isaac are goin' into business together," he say, wave his arm to where Isaac is hunched over a beer in the corner. Pa's eyes move into every corner of the room as he is talking to me. He searches out every dark spot as if he expect somebody to be hiding there with a gun.

"That's nice," I say. I hope my tone let him know I don't want to hear any of the details.

We exchange small talk for a few minutes. Pa eye the beer on our table. I don't offer and he don't have the nerve to ask. Finally he head back over to Isaac.

After he's gone Sadie stay silent, sipping at her beer. She know better than to talk to me about my dad.

When, a while later, Sadie get up to go to the washroom, I see Paul Ermineskin skulk off in that direction, peeking over his shoulder, walking kind of sideways as he's known to do.

"How much did it cost you?" I ask Sadie when she get back.

"What?"

I point across the bar to where my dad got a bill in his hand, waving to catch the waiter's attention.

"How much did he borrow?"

"I gave him two ones," she say in a small voice.

More likely she gave him a five.

"I'm gonna have to start charging for the nice things I say to you."

Sadie glare at me, light up a cigarette.

"You tell me I'm *sweet*," she say. "You never tell me I'm *pretty*."

I don't have an answer for that. She's right. I just don't have the nerve to lie like that, even to please someone I love. Sadie stay mad at me all that night, even sleep at her folks' place instead of with me.

Pa's friend, Isaac Hide, is a bachelor, live in a cabin a mile or so back in the bush. He get some kind of pension for being shot during the Korean War. He claim his health is bad, make a little home brew sometimes that he sell to friends. He ain't a bad man, but he is skinny, and furtive, and have an unwashed smell about him. One winter him and Pa cut Christmas trees and sold them in Wetaskiwin. But soon as they'd make a couple of sales they'd both head for the Alice Hotel bar. By the time they drank up their money, then sobered up, half the trees would have been stolen off their lot.

"I hear your old man and Isaac Hide are going into competition with the Alberta Government Liquor Stores," my friend Frank Fencepost say to me a few days later.

"What they do is no concern of mine. I don't imagine Maurice Red Crow and the guys with big stills are shaking in their shoes. Pa and Isaac will have too much of a fondness for their own product to compete with anybody."

At least they picked a good business to go into. There is always a market for cheap moonshine. A day or two later Frank come by my cabin with a beer bottle half-full of a pale liquid the color of a city snowbank.

"Taste like gopher piss and gasoline," says Frank, "but it got a kick like the time I stuck a screwdriver in an electric socket up at the Tech School."

"I wouldn't drink nothin' my pa had a hand in making," I say. "I've seen too many people go blind from drinking bad home brew."

"Gives a whole new meaning to *blind drunk*," laugh Frank.

Either Pa or Isaac must have some business sense hid deep inside them, for their moonshine business pick up real quick, and, to my surprise they ain't their own best customers. They get a bottle-capper, and from somewhere Pa bought up a few dozen blue bottles, squat and square. He give out samples to the drunks who hang around the Canadian Legion in Wetaskiwin: a lot of them guys have money, own farms and businesses. I finally get talked into tasting some at the pool hall one night; it is sweet and fruity, doesn't taste like something been drained out of a radiator and had yeast added to it. And the blue bottles with the shiny copper cap sure look better than a beer bottle with a cork, which is what the other moonshiners turn out.

Inside of a month Isaac trade off his old rattletrap of a car for a Fargo King Cab truck that only four or five years old. They hire my friend Rufus Firstrider to drive deliveries for them.

"You going to have to incorporate and sell shares," somebody suggest to Pa one evening at Hobbema Pool Hall.

Frank he jump up and start to imitate some of the commercials he seen on TV, like the fat man who sell Chrysler cars, and the man who liked the electric shaver so much he bought the company.

"Compare hangovers," Frank say, pretend he walking toward the camera holding up a bottle. "If Paul and Isaac's Moonshine don't make your head hurt twice as much as the next most popular brand, if one bottle don't make you feel like you swallowed a live jackhammer, we'll give you a bottle of our competitor's moonshine free. Remember, with Paul and Isaac's Moonshine we guarantee you're gonna boogie 'til you puke!" And he point a finger at the imagined camera and wink, while everybody clap their hands.

Pa joke that he gonna hire Frank as a full-time salesman. We make a lot of jokes about that, and everybody have a good time. But I notice Pa's eyes still inspecting every corner of the room. He act nervous and sneaky even when he having a good time.

It is just a day or two later that him and Isaac get a big break. RCMPs, who haven't been bothering moonshiners for a few months, led by Constable Bobowski, the meanest lady RCMP in three provinces, swoop down on Maurice Red Crow's still, what located on a farm up by the town of Kavanagh. They don't catch Maurice, but they haul out two truckloads of equipment, carry it direct to the town dump where a bulldozer trash it good. Maurice will be out of business for quite a while.

Not even a week later Constable Bobowski and her friends hit again; this time they come right on to the reserve, carry off all of Jarvis Lafreniere's equipment, dry stock and bottled goods.

Now everyone know the RCMP can be lucky once.

"But they'd need both the Pope and Pastor Orkin of the Three Seeds of the Spirit, Predestinarian, Bittern Lake Baptist Church on their side for them to make two strikes in a row," say Frank.

"Either that or a snitch," I say. My friends at the pool hall all stop what they are doing when I use that word.

"Come on, nobody on the reserve would do that," say Rufus Firstrider.

There is an unwritten law that say no matter what been done to you, it is a personal matter. We all know that beside a snitch a snake is ten feet tall.

"But there *are* always snitches," says Frank. "If there weren't RCMP would be out of business years ago."

"That's true *off* the reserve," I say. There are guys I know in the cities who make their living as police snitches, though they are frightened all their lives and always about half an inch from being murdered. RCMP are as anxious for a snitch as an alcoholic for a drink. We been known occasionally to set them up by having someone pretend to be a snitch, then give false information.

"But there have been *two* hits," someone say. "RCMP just ain't that smart on their own."

"We'll all have to keep our eyes open," I say, and everyone agree with me.

It was three nights later I stumble on Constable Bobowski doing something strange in the dark. I was walking home from Blue Quills Hall when I seen an RCMP car parked down a side road, lights off and empty. Something must be going on I figure. I follow a path down through a pine grove to where a dry slough form a clearing. It is a cloudy night so I can't see good. But I make out two figures lean on a wire fence; one of them is smoking.

They stop talking once when I kick a root and stumble. I figure anybody who meet at midnight in a secret place is up to no good. I wonder for a minute if maybe Constable Bobowski got an Indian boyfriend, or maybe Constable Chrétien have an Indian girlfriend; that would be more likely.

"What you figure goin' on down there, Chief Tom?" I say real loud, scuff the ground with my feet.

Boy, the person who was smoking crash through that fence, set the barbed wire to zinging, pound off through the bush like a panicked moose.

Turn out that other person *is* Constable Bobowski; she is cool and businesslike.

"What are you doing here?" she ask me.

"I seen the car all locked up. Thought whoever was driving it might be in trouble."

"No. I caught something in my headlights and went to investigate, but it was just an animal. You heard it running away."

We are both pretty good at lying.

"Can I give you a ride to your house?" ask Constable Bobowski. This is the first time she has been nice to me, ever.

In the car I say to her, "You got a cigarette, Constable Bobowski?"

"Sorry," she says. "I don't smoke."

"I didn't think so." And I look a long time at the side of her face.

"There were a lot of fireflies down in the slough tonight," she says as she lets me out of the patrol car.

"Thanks for the ride," I say.

First sign of daylight I'm at the slough. What I find is what I expect to find, a triangle of red-and-white checkered material hanging from one of the barbs, where whoever was with Constable Bobowski crashed through in a hurry. When I see the place in daylight I realize it only about a third of a mile cross country from Isaac Hide's cabin.

What I don't find out until Frank come by my cabin about noon is that sometime around dawn the RCMP hit Isaac and Pa's still, carry off everything including Isaac Hide and my friend Rufus Firstrider.

"Isaac'll get six months or so at the Crowbar Hotel in Fort Saskatchewan," laugh Frank.

"What about Pa? Did they get him too?"

"He was off at his girlfriend's in Wetaskiwin. I was at the pool-hall when she dropped him off about an hour ago. That was the first time he heard of the raid."

"Pa's the snitch," I say to Frank. "Pa's been gettin' paid by the RCMP to sell out both his friends and his enemies."

"You better have some proof of that, Silas. You could get your old man killed. If Maurice Red Crow or Jarvis Lafreniere ever believed that . . . ."

A few nights later, I stick my head in the door of the Trav-elodge cocktail lounge, about the fanciest drinking spot in Wetaskiwin, and there is Pa and Isaac and a couple of women I don't know. Isaac's woman look Indian though she's dressed in expensive clothes, the other woman have yellow hair crinkled tight as a brass kitchen brush, a wide face paved with make up, and big, fat, lipsticked lips.

Pa see me before I can duck out.

"Hey, Silas, come over and meet my friends."

I move slow across the room, until I realize I'm walkin' side-ways, the way Pa does so often. I sure have to watch that. I don't want to inherit *anything* from Pa.

"How come you're not drinkin' your own product?" I say and make a weak smile.

"When you want to read a book, do you read one of your own?" says Pa.

I get introduced to the ladies, but I don't even hear their names.

"What you doing here?" I say to Isaac Hide. I knew they just held Rufus Firstrider overnight and let him go; but Isaac owned the still.

"Your pa here got me a lawyer. I'm out on bail. Lawyer says the seizure was illegal, and that they'll let me go and even have to give back our equipment. A case of the big, ugly RCMP hassling us poor, enterprising Native Canadians," and everybody have a good laugh.

"Sit down, Silas, I'll buy you a drink," says Pa. He is wearing a new buckskin jacket with porcupine quill designs, western-cut pants and new boots.

"I gotta get going."

"Hey, one drink," and he pull out a roll of bills so big it got an elastic around it.

"If you're really feelin' flush," I say, "maybe you could repay the money you stole from your little girl a year or so ago." I say that loud and clear so, if nothing else, I'll embarrass him in front of his ladyfriend.

"You know that was just a loan. I always intended to pay her back."

"Well here's your chance. He stole three hundred dollars from his little girl, money she'd earned for a dance costume," I say right to the yellow-haired lady, in case she don't know how bad a company she keeping. But when I look at her face I see her eyes are close together and there ain't a sign of intelligence in them.

"It was a loan," Pa is saying, and he start counting bills off his roll. The elastic break and zoom over a couple of tables; Pa upset a drink send ice and orange juice in a flood across our table. But he lay out a row of twenties, even add one for interest, though he should add three or four. I fold the bills and stuff them in the front pocket of my jean jacket, close the button with a snap.

"You're welcome," Pa say, and laugh a little, a sound his ladyfriend pick up and echo. I don't look around until I'm out on the street. It sure make Delores happy to get paid back, but somehow I don't feel as good as I think I should.

I get to thinking that I bet the RCMP using the wrong procedure when they raid Pa's still was all part of the deal. Isaac was right and the RCMP truck bring their brewing equipment back to the reserve before the end of the week.

I'm sure surprised when a couple of days later there is a knock at my cabin door, and when I open it there is Pa. He must have watched to be sure Ma and the other kids is out.

"What do you want?" I say. I go back and sit at the table where I been working on a story.

"Just thought I'd come by and see my favorite son."

"Don't try to butter me up. You don't like me any better than I like you. You come by to see if you could steal Delores' money back? She put it in the bank this time where you can't get at it."

"I come by because I hear you've been spreading lies about me."

"What could anyone say bad about you that would be a lie?"

"I hear you callin' me a snitch."

"You are a snitch. I seen you meet with Constable Bobowski."

"You seen me?"

"I found cloth from your jacket on the fence."

"How many guys on the reserve own red-and-white mackinaws?"

"I *know*," I say.

"What is it you do, Silas?" Pa say to me; his eyes meet mine and hold on; it is the first time in our lives we ever looked each other in the eye.

"I ain't no snitch, if that's what you mean. We take care of troublemakers in our own way. We have our own law. We never call in outsiders. And I never snitched to the horsemen in my life."

"You're pretty high and mighty," Pa say. "You and your god-damned stories and books. You're the biggest snitch ever been known on this reserve . . . ."

"Hey, wait a minute . . . ."

"You don't just snitch to the cops, you snitch to the whole world. I've had people read your stuff to me when I was in the joint, and I don't admit I'm related to you. You tell everybody's secrets, no matter how awful or how personal. And you know what the worst thing is? You ain't even successful—I made more money sellin' home brew last week than I bet you make in a year. You ain't even a successful snitch."

I have to admit he's right about the money. I'm still able to draw welfare, even though I got books printed up, and had my picture and a story in the *Edmonton Journal.*

"I only sell doctored water make people forget their troubles for a few hours," he go on. "You pick the scabs off sores."

"And you never beat my mom and us kids. And you never drank up the welfare while we was starving here at home."

"Silas, I done a lot of things I ain't proud of, but if you think I turned in those still owners, turned in my friend Isaac for money . . ." Pa standing at the end of the table looking down at me. When I don't take back my accusation he say, "Well, here," and Paul Ermineskin fumble around under his coat and come out with a sawed-off .22 rifle. He lay it on the table.

A gun like that is about the most illegal thing you can own. I wonder who he stole it off of.

I guess it tell a lot about how I feel about my father, because for half a second I was afraid he was gonna use that gun on me.

"It's for you, Silas," he go on. "If you think I'm an RCMP snitch, the lowest life in the world, if you believe for sure I done it, then you better take your revenge." He stare down at the gun where it sit on the table, the butt turned toward me.

I can already smell the oily metal, the bitter odor of gunpowder.

"Look, Silas, I'm a bad bugger. Everybody knows that, including me. I mean I even stole money from my little girl. I'm sorry for it and I'm glad you made me pay her back. But Silas, I ain't a snitch. I wonder if you really know what happens to snitches. Last time I was in the joint there was this guy—we took him into the welding shop and used a blowtorch on him. Guards rescued him before we killed him, but he'll never be the same. Do you think I'd risk *that*? You name somethin' rotten and I done it, all except snitch to the cops."

"I'll make it easy for you, Silas," he go on, and he reach down into his boot and pull out a hunting knife, one I'm pretty sure used to belong to Adolph One-wound. He grip it like he might attack me. "Pick up the gun and blow me away," he say. "You can say I showed up in an ugly, drunk mood and came for you with this knife and gun. You can claim you took the gun away from me. We even make it look like there been a fight," and he kick over a chair and with his free hand sweep the ashtray and a stack of my books onto the floor.

I'm sure he's a snitch. But not sure enough to take any action. Not that I'd kill him for it anyway.

"No, Pa, even if you done it . . ."

"Silas, I make it even easier for you. If you believe in your heart that I snitched, all you got to do is spin that gun around to face me. I'll take it out to the woods and do the job myself."

"No," I say real loud. "Take your stuff and get out," and I motion to the gun but I don't touch it.

"Don't you bad mouth me no more then. Never say you didn't have your chance." His eyes glow yellow in the lamplight. They are small and deep set but full of victory, like a fighter just scored a knock-out. He pick up the gun, shove it under his jacket, and sidle out the door.

I've had my bluff called. Damn Pa! He'd make a hell of a politician. He don't have the courage for there to have been bullets in the gun. I didn't have the courage to call his bluff. The only thing we agree on is that a snitch is the lowest form of life in this world. We both think of each other as being one. And I guess we ain't likely to change our opinions.

Pizza Ria

C athy Calling Bird is the name get chosen for her, though her real name was Ria Meloche, and she was the sixth of 14 kids raised in a slant-roofed cabin miles deep in the muskeg near the back end of Hobbema Reserve.

Ria Meloche discover when she was about 14 she could sing like a real bird. She start out at talent contests at Blue Quills Hall, imitating Loretta Lynn and Dottie West, plunking away on a $10 guitar that somebody else throwed away.

In no time at all she was singing at Saturday-night dances at the Alice Hotel bar. They say Mad Etta put up the money to buy Ria's first costume: a short red skirt with a red velvet vest over a white blouse, a white cowgirl hat and white boots.

A DJ from CFCW, the country music radio station in Camrose, heard her at the Travelodge lounge in Wetaskiwin, and soon she's singing on the radio. A talent agent in Edmonton hear her and sign her up. They decide in Edmonton Meloche don't sound Indian enough, so they change her name.

She made her first record just over a year ago. It sold real well, and she right away get invited to tour as an opening act for the Statler Brothers. I seen her last month on a TV show come direct from Nashville.

Ordinarily we'd figure we seen the last of Ria-Cathy. It sure is a surprise when a fat envelope arrive for me in the mail, have United States stamps on it and a Los Angeles, California, postmark. Inside is a letter from Ria Meloche along with 16 tickets for a Statler Brothers concert at BC Place in Vancouver.

I didn't even know that Ria ever read my books, but in her letter she say she guesses her and me are the most famous people ever to come out of Hobbema. That make me her fan for life. Usually only famous people anyone can name from Hobbema is a guy who played one game in the NHL about ten years ago, a cowboy who was All-Round at the Calgary Stampede and a man who committed a mass murder on the reserve back in the 1950s.

She tell me her tour ends in Vancouver, and then she gonna work for two weeks in a country cabaret called The Texas Star that supposed to have over an acre of dance floor.

"Sixteen people is just an average load for Louis' pickup truck," grin Frank Fencepost, my closest friend, who been reading that letter over my shoulder.

"We can only take fifteen to the concert," I say. "Mad Etta take up two seats all by herself. And we have to set a skinny person on each side of her as well."

Frank is quick to make a list of who we take along.

"I think Ria might like to see some of her family," I point out. The main memory I have of Ria Meloche is her riding bareback on her pony named Bunty, a little, shaggy-maned pinto her papa must have taken in trade for furs. In her letter she ask about her horse first and her family second. I can still see her in front of Hobbema General Store, her arms around Bunty's neck, feeding him sugar cubes she bought in a flat, white box.

Her parents is true bush Indians. Ria can't even send them a letter 'cause neither one can read or write. Her mama is a short, round lady with big eyes, who seem really shy. Her papa, Baptiste, is a thick-bodied man with big, scarred hands, who wear deerskin pants and moccasins he made himself. They both work all year on a trap line and don't speak one word of English between them. Mrs. Meloche ain't ever been off the reserve in her whole life, and we have to talk quite a while before they agree to go with us. Frank suggest we take Bunty the pony along, and for a while we even consider it.

Ain't hard to fill the truck: there is me and Frank and our girl friends; the Meloches, Mad Etta, Bedelia Coyote, Eathen Firstrider; my girl Sadie's brother David One wound is there. David carry a jack and wheel wrench in a red, silken backpack. He wins bets by stripping cars of all four wheels in under four minutes.

Nobody is quite sure how Father Alphonse from the Reserve School got to go with us. Maybe Mr. and Mrs. Blind Louis Coyote invite him. Father Alphonse is French, might have some Indian blood, might not. He been around the reserve for so long we consider him almost one of us.

"As long as you and the church kick in ten percent of the gas money, you're welcome," say Frank.

The trip out to Vancouver goes pretty smooth. While we filling up at a town called Boston Bar, David One-wound win $5 from Eathen Firstrider by stripping the wheels and the grille off a Buick station wagon that got three little kids and a dog inside it. They was waiting while their mama used a washroom. The truck box got pretty crowded with all those extra auto parts mixed in there with the people.

Blind Louis take out his slingshot, what he made from a solid Y of red willow and a band of brick-colored inner tube. Mrs. Blind Louis tell him where to shoot, and as we drive along through the Fraser Canyon, he fling lug nuts at crows.

Turn out we is a couple of weeks early for the concert, which is on the 31st, not the 13th as we thought. I drive the truck down toward East Hastings Street, where David One-wound, who known as the One-wound Auto Parts Company Limited, going to sell off those wheels and grille, maybe generate some new business so we can all afford rooms in a real hotel.

We hardly get the truck parked when we meet up with our friend Bobby Billy; we find him leaning on the same parking meter as a year ago, when I give a reading at SFU. Bobby Billy look a little worse for wear, and has on only one shoe.

"Did you lose a shoe?" asks Frank.

"No, I found one," say Bobby Billy. His face break open real slow, take about 30 seconds for his whole smile to get in place. "By golly, I heard RCMPs sealed up the border to Alberta to keep guys like you on the other side of the mountains."

Bobby Billy is a BC Indian, come from the big, rainy mountains behind Vancouver.

Bobby is not much taller than the parking meter; he got a wide, pushed-in face, and laces of black hair cover his forehead. He push that hair first to one side then the other, but it always fall back like it was before. He wear a green-and-black plaid shirt, green work pants too big for him, and his one shoe.

"I'm sure glad to see you guys. And yonder big lady, too," he say, make a little bow toward Etta. "I got a serious problem that maybe you can help me with."

"Hey, there is no problem too large for Fencepost the Great," say Frank, slap a hand on Bobby Billy's shoulder. "Pour your heart out, my son."

Etta shove Frank out of the way, and it lucky the store she shove him against was boarded up or he would of been inside.

"You're movin' in on my territory," say Etta. "I'm still the medicine woman around here. Now, what's your problem, Shorty?"

"About four blocks down the drag," and Bobby Billy point east on Hastings Street, "is a place called Guido's Pizza. That restaurant been there for about twenty five years, run by a nice old man from Italy. I been helping him out for ten years or more. I washed dishes when he was busy, even chopped mushrooms for him sometimes. At closing time, Guido would crack open a bottle of wine, him and me would sit and talk all night.

"About a month ago Guido died . . ."

"Went to that big pizzeria in the sky," say Frank, who now is standing behind Bobby Billy where Etta can't reach him.

". . . and he left the restaurant to me," say Bobby. "One morning this big lawyer in a $1,000 suit show up at my place at the Boston Rooms there on Columbia Street, say Guido had no relatives and he left the restaurant to me because I was a good friend to him."

"So why's that a problem?" ask Frank. "You get to eat and drink free forever. Personally, I always dreamed of owning my own 7-Eleven store, so I could go in and hold it up every day."

Frank dance backward along the sidewalk. "Let's not waste time. Let's get down there and open it up. Time is money."

"Time is orange juice," say Frank's girl Connie.

"Time is a moccasin," say Blind Louis.

"What do we know about running a restaurant?" I say to Frank.

"Trust your chef," say Frank.

"Only tool in a kitchen you know how to use is a bottle opener," I say.

Bobby lead us down the street until we see the sign, blue letters on a white background, say GUIDO'S PIZZA. We all press our faces against the windows and peer inside.

"What are we looking at?" ask Blind Louis.

"Is that good to eat?" Mrs. Meloche say in Cree of the line of neon the color of a cardinal that spell out PIZZA in the window.

By the time Bobby Billy, who speak each word like it was water slow-dripping out of a tap, can even start to answer, Frank has opened the door by using the can-opener blade of his jackknife.

Inside it smell spicy. Tied to the top corner of the door is a little fishing bell, which tinkle pretty each time the door open or close.

Frank stare round, then say, "This place hold about ten thousand people." He pause. "If you only let them in sixty at a time."

There is red carpet down the middle aisle from the front door to the waitress station. Three steps lead up to the kitchen. The tables is solid and covered in red-and-white checkered table-cloths. The wallpaper is velvety red, soft to the touch, with a raised, swirly pattern. There is tiny electric candles at about ten-foot intervals along all the walls. In the back corner, behind a red velvet curtain, is what Bobby Billy call the family table, where Guido and his friends used to sit out of sight of customers when business was quiet.

In the kitchen, we all stand around the big, silver, two-decker pizza oven, stare at it kind of awestruck, like it something from outer space been dropped in on us.

"Teach us your secrets, strange person," Frank say to the oven.

Turn out Mad Etta is the only one of us know anything about cooking. We read the menu and see that Guido's only sell pizza and spaghetti. Eathen Firstrider fire up the pizza oven, while several of us clean out fridges and coolers of things blue and green that I'd guess was food a month ago.

We also find a good supply of beer and wine, which Bobby invite us to share while we cleaning up the place.

"Since Guido ain't around no more, we'll change the name," say Frank. "The name Fencepost Pizza appeal to me. But being the *magnanimous* person I am, I'll settle for just an Indian name, say Pow-wow Pizza Parlor."

One of the things Frank does that drive us all crazy is, ever since he learn to read and write, he try to improve his word power. He carry a little word book in his pocket, learn a new one every day, which he try to sneak into conversation. Frank has always been about as subtle as a charging moose.

Etta brew up some bread dough and we take turns at making up pizzas on little square boards, look like flat shovels. But when we try to put the pizza in the oven, it stick to the board, and when we push it off it bunch up in a big, messy lump that stick to the oven floor like glue. We even try cooking one pizza right on the board. The board turn black and the pizza stick to *it*.

(Next day we drop in to a Pizza Patio and find out you sprinkle corn meal on the board; the little corns act like ball bearings and roll the pizza into the oven.)

Just as we get ready to leave that night we get our first customers.

We didn't lock the front door after we came in, and even though only the kitchen lights is on, four people come in, sit down and start looking at menus.

"What should we do?" we ask each other.

"Trust your waiter," say Frank, and he run toward the dining room, trip down the steps from the kitchen, stagger all the way to the table.

"Welcome to Pow-wow Pizza. I'm your waiter, Bucking-off-the-mountain. What can I get you dudes?"

The customers, two couples who probably work in a bank, and been to a book-burning, just stare at Frank with their mouths open. It could be that Frank being dressed in denim with a ten-gallon hat, one braid in front, one braid behind, surprise them a little.

"We're the new owners," say Frank. "We come from Hobbema, Alberta, Canada, where men are men and so are at least half of the women."

"Where's Guido?" someone finally ask.

"Out," say Frank.

"When will he be back?"

"Not for a while."

"How long?"

"A long time."

"How long is that?"

"A real long time," say Frank.

The women are pulling at the men's sleeves.

"I think we'll eat Greek," one man say as they get up.

"Hey, we can cook you something Greeks eat. What do Greeks eat?" say Frank as he follow them toward the door. "Grease! That's where they come from, right? I got twenty years experience cooking with grease. Sit yourselves down."

But those people is pushing at each other to be first out the door.

"The secret of success is to delegate authority," announce Frank, while we all having coffee at somebody else's café.

Frank been reading a book called *How To Be A Millionaire By Age 30*, and I guess that is one of the things he learned.

As Frank pop a set of pepper-and-salt shakers in his pocket, he say to Connie, "For instance, instead of teaching you and Sadie to be waitresses like that girl over there," and he point at a young woman in a pleated yellow miniskirt and brown jumper, have three plates balanced down each arm, "I'd hire her to do a good job waiting tables for us, *and* train you girls at the same time." Frank smile like he just invented something.

When the waitress come to our table, Frank stand up, bow a little, doff his cowboy hat and say, "Hello, beautiful lady, what's your name?"

"Don't even bother," the girl say, scowl at Frank; she is waiting on six tables, all got four or more people at them.

"That must be an Indian name," say Frank. "Allow me to introduce myself: I am Fencepost, president of the Rocky Mountain Multiple Orgasm Society. Actually, I'm looking for Hot To Trot. Have you seen her?"

"Don't pay no attention to him," say Connie Bigcharles, have a good grip on Frank's shoulder to show who he belong to. "He has problems. Last week his mother told him to take out the garbage. He took it out to dinner and then to a dance hall."

"Last night down on Granville Street he see a sign say WET PAINT, so he did," I add.

"I know his type," say the waitress, come close to smiling.

"Seriously," say Frank, "underneath I'm a different guy: shy, sensitive, caring . . ."

"Conniving," say Bedelia Coyote.

"Right. No. Listen. Under this," and he pat his chest, "is a serious person looking for another serious person." He pause. "Under that is two floors of pay parking . . ."

By the time we get to dessert, the waitress, whose name is Tina Louise Bodnarchuk, agree to at least come by Guido's and talk about working for us.

"How come you've got a priest with you?" ask Tina Louise.

"A Fencepost leaves nothing to chance," say Frank.

"I am from the tribe of fishing people," say Bobby Billy in his slow monotone speech. "In my language a priest is the stick we use to club fish to death."

"I've thought of everything," say Frank. "We got a priest to pray for us; a blind man so we can park in the handicapped zones; my friend, Standing-knee-deep-in-running-water here, write books; and they used Mad Etta over there as the model for BC Place."

Mrs. Meloche, who never been in restaurants before, order up three pieces of lemon pie all at once. She ain't caught on that you have to pay for all the food get delivered to your table.

Over the next few days it is Mad Etta who take charge of things, though it is Frank who think he do. Tina Louise does come to work for us, and she train Sadie and Connie to wait tables. The rest of us stay out of sight of the customers.

"Public ain't ready to find fifteen Indians running a pizza place," growl Mad Etta.

"It's like being guards after years of being inmates," say Frank, scratch his head in puzzlement as he sit at our family table, tired, sweaty, and so covered in flour he might pass for a white man.

The first lesson we learn about running a restaurant is to hate the public. Restaurant customers is dirty, ornery, stone-cold thieves, and every one of them splashes when they eat. What they don't spill on the tablecloth they toss on the floor, and if anything's left over they wipe it on the walls.

They steal dishes, glasses, knives and forks, salt shakers and ashtrays. If they thought they could get away with it, they would carry out the tables and chairs.

Late one night we all sitting around the family table. There is only six customers eating at a table by the front window; three sailors and their girl friends. We hear the fishing bell on the front door tinkle, but just barely. Frank put an eye to the slit in the curtains.

"Look at that!" he whisper.

Soon we all peering through that slit. Me at the top, then Frank, Etta, Connie, Sadie and Bobby Billy. What we see is one of them customers untying the bell from the door. He get it loose, peer around like a dog about to steal meat, raise his pant leg and tuck the bell into his sock.

"We gonna serve that dude as ground beef on our pizzas for the next few days," say Frank, rub his hands together. "Let's go pound him good."

But Etta get a grip on Frank's arm so he can only hop up and down on one spot.

"What are you gonna have if you fight?" say Etta.

"A good time," say Frank.

"You gonna have broke furniture and dishes, and you don't collect the check from those guys. You can buy another bell for a dollar."

"Less than that," I say, "but it's the idea."

"Give me the bill," say Etta.

She total up their pizza and drinks, then write, "One Bell, $10," and add it to the total. Etta waddle out with the coffee pot and the bill, ask if they enjoy the pizza, and they say they did.

When they come to pay, one of them notice the added item.

"What the hell's this?" he yell.

"For the bell in your sock," say Etta, smile from way down deep in her face.

"We ain't gonna pay," the sailor say.

"I could call the police," say Etta, "have them look in your sock. Or," and she raise up a heavy black skillet she brought down from the kitchen. "I could teach you guys not to steal."

She smile some more. "Or, you could pay the bill I made out and everyone go home happy."

Them sailors look at Etta, and at me, Frank, Eathen, Bobby, Mr. Meloche and Blind Louis.

"Right you are, Mama," one of them say, and cough up the $10.

The way we learn to do delivery orders was we bought a map of Vancouver, glued it to a piece of cardboard; we put one colored pin where the restaurant sat, another where the delivery supposed to go. Then somebody drive, somebody navigate, somebody keep the pizza wrapped tight in a moose-hide robe.

We also learn fast that on delivery orders we got to take a phone number and call back, because people like to place phony orders.

One night we get a call for four large pizzas; I phone the number myself and a boy's high voice confirm the order. But when we get to the address the people never ordered pizza and they have a different phone number. We go back to the shop, not knowing what to do next.

"The beat cop is a friend of mine," say Bobby Billy. "I bet he could help."

That cop, a Constable Rudd, drop in for free coffee a couple of times a night. Constable Rudd is almost as slow-spoken as Bobby Billy, and has a handlebar mustache that look like a squirrel tail been glued under his nose. He make a call to headquarters and get us the address where that telephone located.

About eight of us show up at the house, where a skinny kid of about 15 with a thin nose and about a pound of acne on his face answer the door. He is real surprised to see us.

"That'll be $45," say Frank, hand him the pizza boxes.

"I didn't order no pizza," he say in that high voice I heard over the phone.

We yell back and forth for a few minutes until the boy's father appear. He look like he could lift Mad Etta if he put his mind to it.

"Is he at it again?" he say to us. Then he pick that greasy kid up by one arm and slam him against the wall. Both the wall and the kid crack a little.

"Did you order this stuff?" the father yell. He have to threaten to slam the kid against the wall again before he admit he did.

"I hope those are big pizzas," the father growl at us. "This punk's gonna eat every crumb of every one, or die trying." Then he pay us our money.

"There's enough there to feed twenty people," say Frank. "We add anchovies to every one before we make the second trip."

We can hear the kid making gagging sounds as his father drag him away.

In a few days we doing a good business for Bobby Billy. We close up the night Ria Meloche sing with the Statler Brothers. We all howl up a storm when she come on stage, and afterwards we go backstage where she say hello to her mama and papa, thank us for bringing them, then spend five minutes asking about her horse.

"Soon as I get a permanent place to live I'm gonna send for Bunty," she say.

"Hey!" say Frank. "How about if some night after work at the cabaret you come down to our restaurant and sing for us?"

We all make agreeable sounds.

"Well, I don't know," say Ria. She look over her shoulder at the man behind her. "I don't think so."

"It appear to me that these days Ria is casting a shadow don't look anything like her," say Frank on the way back to the restaurant.

"A beautiful girl with a coyote's shadow," rumble Etta.

"If you want I could make her come to the restaurant," say Ria's mother in Cree. "We owe that little flat-faced Indian Billy for feeding us."

"We don't want her to do nothin' she don't want to," say Etta, smile at me with one side of her face. Without speaking, Etta and I agree there's not much chance Mrs. Meloche have any influence over Ria anymore.

Bobby Billy sure ain't dumb, just bashful. With Etta's help he catch on quick to running the business. We are about ready to head for home and leave Bobby Billy to become a millionaire, when the city health inspector drop in.

Oh, boy, that health inspector rip us up one side and down

another for about an hour. Guess the place hadn't been inspected for years. It ain't just a matter of cleaning and washing: the kitchen-floor tiles have to be replaced; all the walls have to be painted; an electric dishwasher have to be installed; the water heater have to be replaced because it don't heat the water enough to kill germs; the cooler ain't cold enough and the chimney need replacing. We don't even have to get estimates to know the repairs is more money than we got.

"In the Bible," Father Alphonse begin, "they had plagues and locusts . . ."

"Here they got health inspectors," finish up Frank. "He a first cousin to Mr. Clean, or what?"

The health inspector send us a registered letter, give us 14 days to shape up or close up. We all try to figure ways to make money again. All we can come up with is Cathy Calling Bird.

"If she sang for us for three nights we could make enough money to pay for the repairs. We could put ads in both newspapers, put on a $5 cover charge," say Frank.

We load up the truck and head off again to The Texas Star. But talking to Ria-Cathy mean also having to talk to her shadow. It has a name, Justin Barlow. He is a big, heavy-set guy in satin cowboy clothes. He have sideburns shaped like thick pork chops. He speak in a slow drawl, spend a lot of time pushing his $200 cowboy hat back on his head, mopping his brow with a red handkerchief, and smiling.

Ria tell us Justin Barlow is her manager; she also let us know he played steel guitar for Ray Price's band, the Cherokee Cowboys, until Ray Price retired.

"Y'all got to understand that Cathy can't just go singing any old place at any old time," Justin Barlow say to us.

"She has contracts to honor, recording dates, and I have to decide what's good for her career."

"Friendship don't count?" say Bedelia.

"Something you got to learn, little lady, is that successful people always have hangers-on tryin' to pull them down. The real successful people peel off those hangers-on just like old clothes. What it amounts to is successful people don't need friends. Ain't that right, Cathy?"

"I guess so," Cathy say, but she don't look too happy about it.

This is mid-afternoon in the empty cabaret, which is kind of like a forest at dusk. There is actually a cold breeze inside the building, and that acre of empty tables is like a barren field.

"Perhaps I could be of service?" say Father Alphonse.

We all look at him. Father Alphonse don't want anything as much as just to be useful. He been stuck out on the reserve with us Indians because he wasn't very competent.

"A bishop's kind of like a banker, and some priests with big congregations is as powerful as lawyers or accountants, but if we was to give Father Alphonse a name it would be the Dishwasher Priest," is the way Frank describe him.

"I could speak to her of compassion," say Father Alphonse. "Appeal to her better nature. Point out the God-given opportunity to help her spiritual brothers and sisters in distress."

"Give it a shot, Father," say Mad Etta.

He take Cathy off to a distant table, Father Alphonse gesturing often, wiping sweat from his narrow forehead. Cathy continually shake her head, looking over her shoulder to where Justin Barlow lurk among the musical instruments on the bandstand.

Finally, Father Alphonse give up.

"She'll do it for me," Ria's mama say, and pad over on her

moccasined feet to catch Ria before she get back to the band-stand.

I walk part way with Mrs. Meloche, thinking seriously of stopping her. I sure hate to see this little lady disappointed. Ria's a city girl now, and ain't gonna pay no attention to her mama, who's dressed shabby and smell of campfires.

But she sort of slide away from me and pull Ria down at a table, where they do about three minutes of furious Cree speaking before Ria slam her hand on the table, stand and march away real mad. She talk for a minute to Justin Barlow almost as furiously as she been talking with her mother. She stomp her foot at him and stride back to her mama. They whisper back and forth for a minute. Mrs. Meloche come back to us, say to Mad Etta, "Four nights, any time you want her. Me and Baptiste always pay our debts."

She give a small smile from her round, weather-burned face.

"Ah," say Father Alphonse to Mrs. Meloche, rubbing his skinny hands together, "a mother's touch."

Even after all his years on the reserve Father Alphonse speak only halting Cree, and he speak it with a bad accent. "I suppose you spoke to her of love and loyalty, duty to family and to God," he go on.

"Who is this guy?" Mrs. Meloche say real sharp, as she light up a roll-yer-own cigarette, spit a piece of loose tobacco past the priest's ear.

"Yeah, that's exactly what she did," I break in to tell Father Alphonse. "You wore Ria down, her mother just closed the deal." Father Alphonse smile so hard he almost radiate light.

Because I walked part way with Mrs. Meloche, I was the only one heard the conversation. Boy, I underestimate this lady live all her life in the bush. Guess when you put your life on the line in

40-below weather, have to kill for your food and clothes, you learn to state a case plain, don't worry about hurt feelings. What she said to Ria was, "If you don't help our friend who feeds us, when I get back to the reserve I'll kill your pony."

A Lighter Load

"There are people," says Mad Etta, our medicine lady, "who spend their lives creating bad situations, because the only thing they're good at is making the best of them."

"Is Rickey Westwind one of those?" I ask.

"It beginning to look that way," says Etta, swigging from her bottle of Lethbridge Pale Ale.

"Why do you suppose he come to you in the first place? He never been one to have anything to do with the old ways."

"Guilt works in funny ways. If that's what his problem really is."

That mean Etta don't think guilt is Rickey's real problem. A couple of years ago, I wouldn't have realized that right away. Maybe I am learning something by being her assistant, though she never seems to give me a chance to do much of nothing.

Rickey Westwind just been at Etta's cabin for about two hours. He been, as Frank Fencepost would say, pouring his guts out. Rickey ain't even lived on the reserve for maybe five years. I'd guess him to be 28 years old, a guy everybody predict would be successful, and so far nobody is disappointed. But they will be if he tells the world what he told Etta here tonight. Rickey worked for a bank for a few years after high school, learn to do accounting. He dress in suits and ties, smell like a bouquet of flowers all the time. He live in Wetaskiwin, marry himself a white girl; they got twin daughters, and he went to work for Department of Indian Affairs a couple of years ago, have a job to do with giving out grant money for construction projects.

It was sure a surprise when Rickey come driving up to Etta's cabin in his big wine-colored Buick. He put on khaki pants and a plaid sports shirt, guess so he figure to look more Indian, but, like all his clothes, they appear perfectly clean, like they never been worn before. Rickey is thin and sink-chested, his hands are long and bony, he have a thin mustache and black eyebrows that stand out on the yellowish skin of his forehead.

"I've done something real bad," he tell Etta.

"There are degrees of bad," says Etta. "You hit-and run somebody? Stole a steak from Safeway? Killed your wife and kids?"

"I've stolen," he said. "Well, not really. I took money to let somebody know about bids on a construction deal. Then I let them put in a lower bid."

"Who really got hurt?" ask Etta.

Rickey Westwind pause for what must be a full minute, before he say real quietly, "Me."

It turn out that some sneaky friends of Chief Tom Crow-eye was behind the trouble. Gerald Proulx and Augustus Fryingpan from the reserve, and Lucien Benoit, who is only a Metis, live in Edmonton and own a big construction company. They gave Rickey Westwind and his assistant Peter Cougar $5,000 each to fix the contracts.

"What should I do?" Rickey ask Mad Etta.

"I think you got something in mind already," says Etta. "Before you do anything consider careful about who got hurt. The original low bidder lost out, but he don't know that. Indian Affairs actually saved money by getting a lower bid. You and Peter Cougar got some extra money. What you did ain't honest, but it wasn't hurtful. If you feel real bad about it, I'd suggest you take the money and give it to a charity: Bedelia Coyote set up a shelter in Wetaskiwin to help battered women and kids. I think that would make everything even. Learn from your mistake and don't do it again."

It plain from the way Rickey Westwind was fidgeting around while Etta talking that he ain't interested in what she is saying.

Etta sigh big.

"What is it *you* want to do?"

"I'm going to the RCMP and confess everything."

"You got a real sore conscience, eh?"

"Yeah," say Rickey.

"You gonna hurt a lot of people if you do that. I hear you got a nice wife and some pretty kids. What about your assistant? Shouldn't he have a say in whether you go to the police?"

"I've gotta do it, no matter."

"Lucien Benoit and those friends of Chief Tom are big-time crooks. They might kill you to keep you from testifying."

"I gotta do it. I got to make things right."

Etta sigh again.

"Has the church got anything to do with this?" she ask. "You believe those devils the Catholics always pushing gonna burn your hide if you don't come clean?"

"Not really. I was fed that stuff as a kid. But I got to confess for myself."

"What you doing is taking a light load and turning it into a heavy one. Not the other way around. Only person who is going to get any satisfaction from you confessing, is you."

"If that's true, I'll just have to live with it."

"You'll be kind of a hero, you know. Is that what you're after?"

"A hero?"

"Sure. You'll drag down those friends of Chief Tom, maybe even the chief himself, if he ain't kept his hands snowy-clean."

"No. I don't care about anybody else. I got to square myself with the world."

"That's what I was afraid of," say Etta. "You know there are some people who are only happy when they're unhappy?"

"I'm not one of them." Rickey get up off his chair. "I'm sorry I come. I thought you'd be happy I want to be an honest man."

"Only if it done for the right reasons. When are you planning on going to the RCMP?"

"First thing in the morning."

"Have you told your wife yet?"

"No."

"Don't you think you owe it to her?"

"What difference would it make?"

"Maybe not much to you, but a lot to her. And what about your assistant? I know Peter Cougar. He ain't smart enough to do anything crooked. You got to prepare him. If you don't do it, I will."

"I'll talk to him," Rickey said reluctantly.

"No. Silas will stop by his place and bring him over here. Tonight. You go home and sleep on your idea. You don't go to the police until we talk again."

Etta indicate by a wave of her hand that his time with her is over, and Rickey Westwind let himself out the door. It easy to tell he ain't used to being waved out doors.

"Don't just sit there," say Etta to me, "get over to Peter Cougar's. If he ain't home, wait for him, and bring him back here."

Peter is a year or two older than me. He still live with his folks here on the reserve. He is barrel-chested, with a wide, flat face. He wear black suits, and black-rimmed glasses. His eyes are big and sad and he puff when he walk fast, a little like Etta, who puff when she walk, period.

I find Peter at home. I call him out on the porch, say I have something private to tell him.

"What do you suppose Old Etta want with me? I hardly know her," he say.

"Probably just wants a share of the bribe money you took," I say real casual. I never seen anybody sweat instantly before. His face bead up and his breath get short, all at the same time.

"Nobody was supposed to know," he whisper.

"Everybody *always* knows about something like that," I say. "Don't worry though, Etta probably only wants a cut. Etta is kind of like the church: If you pay her off she'll leave you alone; if you don't pay, she'll be on your back like a bobcat."

Peter is a real pain in the ass; by the time Etta talk to him for a few minutes he is in tears. She is real patient with him, though. If Frank was here he'd just say "If you can't do the time, don't do the crime."

"I don't want to go to jail," Peter sob. "I don't want to lose my job. I didn't want to do it in the first place, but Rickey made me," and he go to snuffling some more. "Why is he going to the police? He was the one real anxious to take the money. He can't do that.

Lucien Benoit and his friends will kill us both." He even go and stand beside Mad Etta, who perched way up on her tree-trunk chair at the back of her cabin, actually cry on her shoulder.

"You go and see Rickey tonight," she tell Peter. "Silas will go with you to make sure you say the right thing. You tell him you need a week to decide what to do. If he's going to confess you might want to be in Toronto, or someplace just as far away when he make his confession."

"I got a cousin in Washington State," sniff Peter.

"Go sit in the truck. Silas will come out in a minute," she say.

"What if Rickey won't give him time?" I say.

"He will," say Etta, "and if he'll give one week he just might give another, and by then he may come to his senses. There ain't nothing as sad as a guy who wants to clear his conscience and take everybody down with him."

Rickey do give the extension, but over the next few days both him and Peter hover around Mad Etta's like a couple of crows waiting for food. Etta try to talk turkey with Rickey Westwind, but he insist he have to confess so he can live with himself.

"Hmmmph," is all Etta says. But if you know Etta, you know it could take a politician six days of steady talking to say the same thing.

The morning of the fifth day, Etta say to me, "Go tell Rickey Westwind to come up here on his lunch hour. I used up all my speechmaking on him last night. Today I take action. After you tell him, you drive into town and bring his wife and kids out here. I want them to see what kind of a faker he really is."

Rickey's wife, who is a plain-looking white girl, name of Jennifer, ain't thrilled to ride to the reserve with a strange Indian in a truck held together by rust. But when I tell her it have to do with Rickey, and how the only person in the world likely to convince him not to confess is Etta, she put on a bright green jacket have her name on the sleeve and "Senior Women's Softball" on the back in gold letters, bundle the kids into the truck with me.

"He what!" is the words Rickey yell when Etta tell him her piece of news. Then he repeat it, "He what!"

"You heard me," say Etta. "You been saved a whole lot of trouble. Peter Cougar went to the RCMP this morning and confessed everything. You won't have to worry anymore; it may take a day or two, but the RCMP will be around to arrest you."

"You crazy old woman," Rickey shout. "You had him do this, didn't you?"

"The idea did cross my mind," say Etta. "Guess Peter Cougar must of read my thoughts." And she smile like that Mona Lisa picture.

"Don't you realize what you've done!" Rickey go right on yelling. "They'll make a hero out of him. He'll get his wrist slapped, maybe not even get fired. I'll get dragged in just like a cheap crook. It'll look like I was trying to keep the money instead of give it back."

His voice run down like a record player been unplugged. If Etta wasn't so much bigger than him, I'm sure he'd attack her.

"And," he carry on, "they . . . Lucien Benoit and his friends, may think I put Peter up to it. They know he's too stupid to think for himself."

Rickey is pacing around the cabin.

"What I'm going to have to do," he say, as if he talking to people who aren't there, 'cause right now he sure ain't interested in me, or his family, or Etta, "is deny, deny, deny. There was never anything written. If we all stick together we can make Peter look like an idiot, which he is."

"Come to think of it," say Etta. "I may have got my information wrong. You know how old women are. I think it tomorrow that Peter Cougar going to the police. You still got time to beat him to it."

I can see that pale white woman, who done nothing so far but sit at Etta's kitchen table and smoke a cigarette, kind of expanding. She glaring at Rickey Westwind, got a crease between her brows look like she been tomahawked.

This time he don't say "What!" to Etta's statement. He heard her clear enough.

When I was a kid one time, Ma bought from the Goodwill for ten cents, a plastic clown tall as me, that you blowed up full of air. There was sand in the bottom so us kids could punch it hard on the nose and it would rock backward and bounce upright again. I played with that clown for a week or more, until one day my friend Frank Fencepost borrowed a .22 rifle from Louis Coyote's cabin and shot that clown right through the nose. After it was shot it lost its air slowly, taking maybe a minute to sink down until it was just a puddle of airless plastic on the floor.

Rickey Westwind has had the air shot out of him, just like my toy clown. And gonna take years to plug up the bullet holes.

"Hmmmph," say Etta, don't need to be translated.

I got the feeling Bedelia Coyote's charity going to get two big donations later this week.

The Miss
Hobbema
Pageant

We thought it was going to be a problem when my friend, Frank Fencepost, decide to enter the Miss Hobbema Beauty Pageant, but it wasn't until the pageant was over and Frank already lost, that things get sticky.

"Why in the world do you want to enter a beauty contest?" I ask Frank.

"Why not?" say Frank. "There's a $500 dollar cash prize. Winner get to compete in the Miss Indian America Contest going to be held in Edmonton end of the month, right up on the stage at the Circus there in West Edmonton Mall."

"But you're not a Miss!"

"A Fencepost never worry about trivial details. That's why I got you as a friend. You worry enough for both of us. Besides, you ever seen any ads for the Mr. Hobbema Beauty Pageant?"

I have to admit Frank is right about the contests being only for girls.

"I'm a equal-opportunity beauty pageant contestant," says Frank.

We just been to Robinson's Stores in Wetaskiwin, with our girlfriends, where Frank pick up an entry form along with a couple of five-finger bargains. On the entry form where it says, Name? he fill in: FRANKIE FENCEPOST. Then he lie about everything else on the form, especially his measurements.

"You're almost six feet tall; you got a mustache, and you ain't developed in the right places," we remind him.

"Half the girls in Hobbema got mustaches, and those are the good-looking ones," says Frank, dodge a slap from his girlfriend, Connie Bigcharles. "I'll just comb out my braids, put on a pair of pantyhose, strap my friend Cochise here to my leg, and I'm in business."

"You just want to use the same dressing room as the other contestants," I say.

"Hey, nobody should be shy," says Frank. "I been to bed with all but two of the contestants anyway. We got no secrets from each other."

I guess he forgot his girlfriend was there. He glance over at Connie, smile like a dog been caught sucking eggs.

"Just kidding," he say, smile pretty weak. "Not that a lot of these girls don't throw themselves at me. But a Fencepost is able to turn aside temptation . . . ."

"No problem," says Connie, reach over, grab the knife that Frank always wear on his belt. Frank dance backward down the street, just out of Connie's reach. "I just perform a little operation," says Connie, "make you fully eligible to be Miss Hobbema."

It take an hour or so before they make up. Connie has a good heart; she know Frank like her best or he wouldn't keep coming back. But nothing we say can stop Frank from entering the contest. And a few days later when the pageant people realize Frank ain't a girl, they are only able to make a lot of noise, because Frank, he read the rules careful and there ain't a thing say the contestants have to be female.

If there was a panel of judges, like in most beauty contests, Frank wouldn't stand a chance, but the Miss Hobbema Pageant is decided by the general public buying tickets at 50 cents each, the money go to provide sports and recreation, buy craft supplies, help run a daycare center at Blue Quills Hall. When it come to buying tickets people ain't shy, and surprisingly, I can only remember once when the prettiest girl didn't win the contest, and even then it was close.

One year Rider Stonechild come back from working up north on construction, buy $300 dollars worth of tickets for his ugly daughter Brenda. The reason she is ugly is she look just like her dad. But that make other people work harder and Cindy Claw, who is as pretty as any girl on the reserve, win Miss Hobbema that year.

The winner, though I guess she always been eligible, never gone on to the Miss Indian America Contest, 'cause there never been money to send her far away. And past pageants ain't always been well organized. Two years ago, the Hobbema Chapter of the Ermineskin Warrior Society print up three-color posters and distribute them as far away as Edmonton. But that was about all they did. A few hundred people show up for the celebration. But as Frank say, "Whole day was kind of run on Indian Time."

There was a big pow-wow in Saskatchewan that weekend so all our dancers were away; instead of Molly Thunder's Dancing Troupe which is called the Duck Lake Massacre, there is one hoop dancer, Gatien Fire, who is about 60 years old, and wasn't a good dancer even when he was young.

They advertise canoe races, but we haven't got either a lake or a river on the reserve. So the races have to be held on the slough down the hill from our cabins. The slough got about an inch of green stuff on top, look like muskeg moss, and when the racers dip paddles in what pass for water, they come up pretty muddy.

Also, the only dignitary they could get was Mr. J. William Oberholtzer, the ex-mayor of Wetaskiwin who, when he was mayor, wouldn't have come to the reserve if we held a gun to his nose. But being out of politics for a couple of years make him anxious for a crowd to bore.

There are six girls and Frank in the contest, including Melody Crying-for-a-vision, who got to be the prettiest girl, white or Indian, within 50 miles of Hobbema. What happens is that every contestant and their friends go around selling tickets to everybody else. Half the people in the Alice Hotel bar and the Gold Nugget Café have booklets of tickets sticking out of the pocket of their jean jackets.

Soon as they see Frank ain't going to change his mind, our girlfriends get right into the act. Connie Bigcharles get some Super Glue and with a big pair of scissors cut Frank some breasts from the inside of a sofa cushion. One turn out a lot larger than the other, but don't look too awful after the girls strapped him up in a brassiere.

All this happened a couple of months ago and I think Frank still picking bits and pieces of sofa stuffing off his chest. Whoever named Super Glue sure knew what they was doing.

Almost everybody, except the other contestants, like the idea of Frank. He get himself a couple of dresses from the Goodwill Store, a green cocktail dress with fuzzy green trim, and a peach-colored evening gown. People who know him buy lots of tickets because he give them a good laugh, but what turn things in his favor is we go door-to-door in Wetaskiwin selling tickets. White people ain't used to Indians coming to their door, but they sure surprised when six of us show up on their porch, the leader wearing a dress, a cowboy hat, lipstick and a mustache. They buy a couple of dollars of tickets just to be sure we go away.

There never been so big a crowd out to Blue Quills Hall as the night of the pageant. I feel a little sorry for the girls when everybody line up on stage, 'cause the audience all seem to be there to cheer Frank. Except for knobby knees and being a little thick in the waist Frank look pretty good in a bathing suit, and when it is his turn, he parade across the stage, high-stepping like a majorette. The rudest guys in the audience, the rodeo riders like Eathen Firstrider, and Simon Sixkiller, holler out, "Show your tits!" And Frank peel down the front of his bathing suit give them all a cheap thrill. And all the rodeo guys buy maybe $20 dollars each in votes from the Blue Quills Ladies Auxiliary, who stationed around the hall, wearing blue aprons and holding fistfuls of tickets.

There is sure a lot of strange Indians around Blue Quills Hall. I heard that some come from as far away as Great Slave Lake and even Manitoba for this here contest. I don't know what they feed them that they grow so big, but, boy, there is a couple of strange Indians about seven feet tall, lean near the stage, make dents in whatever they lean on. They eye the contestants.

One nod his head toward Frank. "Say, George, you ever seen anything so ugly this side of the stockyards?"

"I think I'm in love, eh?" say George. "I like ugly women. They're easy to catch. Once you got one they try harder. And they never get mad when you fool around on them; they just glad to have you come home at all."

The first guy point at Frank again. "*That one* you couldn't even drink pretty."

But George is in love.

"Hey, sweetheart, I got something to show you I bet you'd like," George say as Frank and the other contestants parade down off the stage.

Frank suggest that George do something to himself that ain't humanly possible.

"I like a woman plays hard to get," says George, blow Frank a big kiss.

"What are you going to do for talent?" I ask Frank, right after he paraded across the stage in his green fuzzy dress, shimmy his backside at the audience who howl like he did something funny. There's no explaining why people get all happy when they see a guy dress up like a girl.

"That is a problem," say Frank. "Guess this audience ain't ready for me to display my real talent," and he grin evil. Frank like to tell the story, though I'm not sure it's true, of how he went into Mr. Larry's Men's Wear in Wetaskiwin, the snottiest, most expensive store within 50 miles, and Mr. Larry, who got a voice that could lubricate cars, say to him, "What's your pleasure, sir?"

"Sex with pretty girls, and driving hot cars," say Frank. "But I'm just here to look for a ten-gallon hat."

Frank and me try to figure out how you display to an audience your ability to con people.

"Maybe I could show how I stuff five-finger bargains down the front of my jeans and boogie out of a store."

We puzzle over that for a while until Frank decide his talent will be storytelling. Two of the girl contestants do the chicken dance, one twirl a fire-baton, would have done her costume a certain amount of damage if it hadn't been fireproof. Another one sing a Loretta Lynn song, and the last one do gymnastic exercises, look like she could tie herself in a bow if she set her mind to it. When it's Frank's turn, this is the story he tell:

"Last year on the July first weekend in Edmonton, I meet this really pretty girl. It is Friday afternoon and after I tell her I'm one of these rich Indians got more oil-money than brains, we go down to Edmonton Motors, where I pick out the hottest car on their lot; I have them make out the registration form in her name, put every extra except manned space flight on it. Then I write that car dealer a check for the full amount.

"'This is Friday,' the dealer say, 'no way to clear the check until Tuesday.'

"'No problem,' I say. 'We just come back Tuesday morning. You make sure she's got a full tank of gas, eh.'

"Tuesday morning I drop by, just in case there's been a mistake, but there hasn't. The check bounced all the way to Wetaskiwin and back and is still quivering on the salesman's desk.

"'If you knew you had no money why did you write the check?' that salesman ask me.

"'For one hell of a weekend,' I tell him."

When they tally up the votes, Frank brought in a record amount of money, have almost double the runner-up, Melody Crying-for-a-vision.

Chief Tom Crow-eye, looking kind of sick, shake Frank's hand, make a point of *not* kissing him, plop on his head the cardboard crown been sprayed with silver paint and sparkles, that make Frank Miss Hobbema.

Frank, who always been one for surprises, make a real nice speech, leave everybody happy.

"It's especially hard for a Fencepost to be humble," Frank begin, "but I want to thank everybody for voting for me. I'm glad we raised a lot of money for a good cause—my prize money. And that's all I'm gonna take is the money. I settle for being first runner-up in this here contest." And while people cheer louder than ever, Frank walk across the stage and put the crown on the head of Melody Crying-for-a-vision.

Miss Hobbema Pageant was one thing but Miss Indian America is another. That contest held over a two-day span at West Edmonton Mall, a place that got about a thousand stores, a carnival, a zoo, and an ice rink all under one roof. Frank describe West Edmonton Mall as "Ten acres of plastic Indian jewelry and french fries." We are there just like big dogs; it impossible to keep Frank away from a place where there's gonna be the 20 prettiest Indian girls in North America competing for a prize.

Soon as we get there this tall, beautiful Indian girl come toward us; she have hair down to her belt, wear a white blouse show off her coffee-colored skin.

"Excuse me," say Frank. "I'm just a poor but handsome Alberta Indian, and I realize we're from two different worlds . . ."

"At least," say the girl, swivel around and leave Frank talking to empty space.

The people who organizing Miss Indian America is from the United States and is professional Indians, in every sense. In charge are Joe Evening and Princess Paula Three Stars. Reason they chose Edmonton was the owners of the mall agree to pay all the expenses for the contest.

After we get a look at the organizers, Frank he say, "I bet Joe and Paula there wear buckskin pyjamas to bed."

Joe Evening probably have some Indian blood in him, but we'd all bet money that Princess Paula Three Stars come from New York City and used to be in advertising. She dress the way people in foreign countries think an Indian should: in plastic beads, imitation buckskin, and moccasins made in Korea.

All the time the Miss Hobbema Pageant going on, Bedelia Coyote and her friend Constable B.B. Bobowski have their noses turned way up in the air, as they always do. They each memorized a page from Ms. magazine about how beauty pageants exploit women, and they repeat that little speech every time they get a chance. What we forgot was that Melody Crying-for-a-vision was a friend of theirs. She was in the Miss Hobbema Pageant for the money, just like Frank. But when it come to other things she have a mind of her own.

And how her mind thinks start to show up the first day of Miss Indian America when all 20 contestants show up for a press conference. Everyone except Melody Crying-for-a-vision is decked out in what the contest call "Traditional Indian garb."

Miss Hobbema is wearing a canary-yellow dress, with a black belt and black shoes, and a big yellow bow in her hair. She stand out among all the artificial buckskin and plastic wampum, like a yellow flower on a brown hillside.

Princess Paula Three Stars is quick to point out that every contestant is to be judged on her "authenticity of traditional dress, knowledge of Indian culture, traditional craft, and modern talent."

"Where does it say I can't wear a pretty dress?" Melody want to know.

"You'll wear what we tell you to wear and nothing else," say Princess Paula.

"Hey," say Frank, who been eavesdropping, "we was at this trade show a few weeks ago, where they elected a Miss Relocatable Structure of America."

"So?" say Princess Paula, stare at Frank like she's spoilin' for a fight.

"So a relocatable structure is a portable outhouse, right. The point is this Miss Relocatable wasn't wrapped in toilet paper, and she sat on a regular chair not a two-holer Johnny-on-the-spot."

"Listen, if I want any advice from you, cowboy, I'll send up smoke signals."

Instead of going bare-knuckle with her as I would of expected, Frank he back off, while Princess Paula turn her attention back to Miss Hobbema, tell her in no uncertain terms that she better dress like everybody else or they disqualify her.

"See, I've learned to take criticism," say Frank, puff out his chest, "instead of assault, now I just think bad thoughts and plot revenge."

"Don't you threaten me," is what Melody Crying-for-a-vision say to Princess Paula. "I'll wear whatever I please whenever I please. And once Miss Hobbema, always Miss Hobbema, you can't do a damn thing to me." Behind her Bedelia Coyote and Constable Bobowski, who is on her day off and dressed like a regular human being in jeans and red sweater, nod their heads and smile.

Some of the reporters there heard most of the kerfuffle, and in the next morning's *Edmonton Sun* is a headline: INDIAN QUEEN BUCKS TRADITION, IRKS OFFICIALS.

Buckskin isn't for Melody Crying-for-a-vision, 19, who says she's been asked to step down as the Miss Hobbema entry in Miss Indian America because she prefers modern dresses to traditional Indian garb. Pageant officials were apparently angry because she wore a conventional dress to a press conference kicking off the two-day contest. Crying-for-a-vision, a member of the Dakota Band on the Ermineskin Reserve, south of Edmonton, said the organizers gave her 24 hours to conform or step down because she won't be a pow-wow princess. She vowed not to resign.

The three judges for Miss Indian America are Jacques Raute, a hockey player who might be one-quarter Indian, used to be third-string goalie for the Montreal Canadiens; a lady with her own afternoon TV show who wear a pound or so of make-up on her face and whose favorite word is *cute*, and a DJ name of J. Paul Bunyan, who over the air, sound 21 and handsome, but in person is at least 45 with a pot-belly and look like he scrunched about 400 years of hard living into his life so far.

There is a big breakfast for all the contestants and the first contest events scheduled for the afternoon. All the contestants except Melody wear their Indian get-ups to breakfast; Melody have on a red blouse the color of a cardinal and a white pleated skirt.

Frank only have to tell a couple of lies to get us in to the breakfast. The white people who work here are a little scared of Indians and tend to believe Frank when he say we are from the Indian TV Network.

"I am Fencepost, TV director to the stars," Frank say to the girl in the red jacket who collecting tickets for the breakfast. "I left our tickets in our room . . . ." Before the girl can say anything Frank stare into her face, step back so he can get a closer look. "You're exactly the type we're looking for," he say. "We need a white girl for that series we going to start filming next week." He turn to me.

"My assistant, Silas Standing-around-with-wet-clothes-on," is how Frank introduce me. "Silas, give this here future TV star our room key so's she can audition right after breakfast."

Guess Frank forgot we slept in the back of Louis Coyote's pickup truck in the parking lot last night.

"I left the key in the room, sir," I say.

"Well, never mind, Room 405, soon as breakfast's over," and we push past and find a seat across from Melody and Bedelia.

We hardly dug into the grapefruit when both Joe Evening and Princess Paula Three Stars bear down on our table.

"Either you dress according to the rules or you're out," snap Princess Paula. Behind her Joe Evening nod his head.

"We've checked the rules," says Bedelia, "there is nothing says she has to wear Indian clothes, in fact," Bedelia go on, smiling kind of sly, "there's nothing says she has to be a girl."

About this time the three judges appear, led by J. Paul Bunyan.

"We've talked this over and we can't see any reason why Miss Crying-for-a-vision can't dress as she pleases," says J. Paul.

Well, Princess Paula turn on the judges, and if her eyes was machine guns she'd mow down all three of them. Up close I can see that it is cherry-colored make-up make Princess Three Stars look like an Indian.

"Listen, you three can be replaced just by my snapping my fingers; there are lots of has-beens and freeloaders who'd kill for a little publicity. You think there aren't a few dozen alcoholic ex-athletes, over-the-hill TV hosts, and sex-maniac disc-jockeys who like to pat a little ass back stage, just waiting for your jobs?"

The three of them shrug their shoulders and retreat, but their eyes are hard.

Princess Paula give Melody one last chance which Melody don't take.

"Alright, we've had enough of your defiant attitude. You're out of the competition. The first runner-up will become Miss Hobbema."

None of us do anything but smile secret smiles. We want to wait until everything is official before we introduce Princess Paula to the new Miss Hobbema.

And with the judges feeling as they do toward the organizers, it not too hard for me to guess who they going to elect as the next Miss Indian America.

Forgiveness
Among Animals

On the night Freddy Powderface began circling his cabin, trotting round and round in a circle pure as if it been drawn for him, I'm sure I was the only person on the reserve who knew what he was up to. He started his run about five in the afternoon, jogging in an even, relaxed way, always staying the same distance from the house whether he passing the front, back, or sides.

I wasn't there for the first half hour or so of his circles. I was down at Hobbema Pool Hall shooting a game of eight-ball with Eathen Firstrider when my friend Frank Fencepost come running in.

"There's about twenty people up at Freddy Powderface's place," Frank puffed. "I always figured Freddy was eight cents short of a dollar, but now he's taken to running in circles around his cabin. Not only that but he's runnin' right through the briars and nettles and he's cutting himself all to rat shit. Looks like he's spent two hours in a bagful of bobcats, or," and here Frank smile his happiest smile, "he look like he spent a night with a girl I knew over to

Duffield Reserve, name of Marion Youngdancer. She raked my back with her nice long fingernails every time she come. And you know me, if a girl come less than twenty-five times I figure I'm losing my touch. But even after that night I didn't look as bad as Freddy does, and I had fun getting my scratches."

Frank, without knowing it, has hit on part of the reason Freddy is behaving like he do. A woman. Or, as it turn out, two women. One is Freddy's wife, Isobel. The other is named Cleo Fire.

Everybody from the pool hall troop up the hill to have a look, and sure enough, everything that Frank said was true. I been expecting Freddy to do *something*, but what he's chosen to do come as a surprise to me, though if I'd thought it through carefully it wouldn't have.

We ain't the only ones who is curious. For whatever reason, people like to watch when somebody doing something weird, so there must be 200 of us there to gape at Freddy.

Freddy's house sit all by itself in front of a poplar grove about a mile up the hill from Hobbema General Store. The house was built by Indian Affairs Department and at one time was painted white on top and kind of a fuchsia-pink on the bottom, but over the years the paint and even some of the siding peeled off. Freddy and Isobel Powderface been living there for maybe three years and got at least that many kids with another one on the way.

The dirt in front and to one side of the house is packed hard from where Freddy parks his car and from people walking and kids playing: nothing grow there but some two-inch-high pigweed and bits of creeping charlie. At one end of the house is a door with a woodpile outside and a path to an outhouse. Nobody been behind the house for years. Back there was waist-high raspberry canes and wild grasses, including some deep green sting nettles tall as a man.

I was sure surprised to see Freddy lope into that mess at his natural speed. He wear mud-colored track pants, running shoes, and no shirt. The raspberry spines rake his skin and the nettles scorch him every pass he make. But Freddy don't change speed or let on that those hurts bother him none.

There is bright blood on Freddy's chest and arms, and even his face have nettle burns on it. After the first hour his track pants is torn and covered with burrs and thorns. The cloth is bloodstained in a lot of spots too. But I can see by standing at one corner of the house, where I can get a good look at the briars he running through, that the worst is over. He gradually breaking a path through that thicket. In a few more hours the raspberry vines won't be clawing at him no more.

Freddy and me got to know each other because he took a course at the Tech School one winter. He was studying biology and have it in his head that he'd like to be a veterinarian some day. But he give up on the courses before long.

"They don't teach nothing practical," he say to me one noon-hour. "I know more animal medicine than the vets who teach these courses. I know more about animals, too."

I explain all the stuff counselors tell us, that if you want a good job you have to put up with the stupid bureaucracy, dumb courses and instructors, until you get that magic diploma. But Freddy wasn't interested and he drop out of school the next week. He do come around and visit me though, which is how I come to know about his troubles, and the reason he decide to run in circles around his cabin.

Freddy sat a broken-backed kitchen chair about 50 feet from his front door. The padded back been lost and the chrome posts look cold and rusty. The seat got a three-cornered tear in it, and when the wind blow, bits of stuffing float off like dandelion fluff.

He rest for about 15 minutes of every hour, have something to eat, a drink, a cigarette, head off to the outhouse. He pay the Coldwind twins to keep him supplied with food, coffee, and such. After the first couple of days he use most of his break-time for sleep. He just drop onto the chair, legs stretched out, shoulders against the chrome posts, put his chin down on his chest and sleep until his helpers wake him up. By taking breaks that way he get about five hours sleep a day, and I hear him tell Carolyn Coldwind, when she deliver him a six-pack of Coca-Cola, that he figure he can keep jogging for six months at least.

By the end of the first week everyone who interested been by to have a look at Freddy. His path is clear now, the scratches on his body is healing and his feet beat a noticeable path into the earth that get deeper with every circle he make. The crowds thin out to almost nothing: they find that watching a guy tromp in circles ain't very exciting. He ain't racing against anybody; there don't appear to be nothing at stake. People stand along the road for a while, or just sit in their cars and stare. Some come by at night after the bars close, shine their headlights on the cabin, pick up Freddy's shadow as he trot by. But it is a little like sitting by the airport to watch planes land and take off; people get bored real quick and go away.

The one person who appear totally uninterested in what Freddy is doing is his wife, Isobel. She ain't even curious enough to pull back the curtains and see what he's up to. They say that about every third day, in a time when Freddy is sleeping, she come out of the house, her arms full of babies, and take the car down to Hobbema to buy groceries. One afternoon when Frank and I was there, his oldest kid, a little girl whose hair hadn't been combed for a couple of days, come out the side door, bare-chested like her daddy, and run a couple of circles with him before her mother call her back inside.

Isobel is a big woman, taller than Freddy, who is skinny with hair wild as twitch grass. She is big-boned, wide of face and body. I've spoke to her a few times at Hobbema General Store or at the Gold Nugget Café in Wetaskiwin, and she seem a nice woman, slow spoken and patient with her babies.

Even after a couple of weeks I still seem to be the only one who know that the reason Freddy is running in circles is that he want his wife to forgive him. There is a long story as to why he believes his wife will forgive him if he run around their cabin long enough. It have to do with badgers.

Freddy Powderface always been full of stories about badgers. I never quite understand how he come to care so much about them ugly, bad-tempered little animals.

"They is just glorified groundhogs," I said to him once.

"Oh, no, no," he say back. "Badgers are special animals. They're smart. Let me tell you some of the stories my grandfather, Powder Horn, the old-time chief, told me before he died. He was a Worthy Man, the last President of the Badger Society."

Then he tell me a story about badgers. Actually he tell me about ten stories about badgers. Trouble is they all sort of blend together after a while. I've never been big on legends, either the white man's or Indian's. They have a sameness about them. First he tell about how a smart badger trick the otter into cutting its own throat. Then he tell how another smart badger lead some starving hunters to where the buffalo are. There are stories of how

Badger outsmart Crow and Raven and Coyote. There is even a story of a grateful chief give Badger his most beautiful daughter. The daughter and the badger produce Indians who is brave and smart and loyal. Freddy stop that last story before he get to the ending, I guess because he can see me yawning.

"Powder Horn predicted the exact hour of his own death," Freddy told a bunch of us at noon hour at Tech School one day, letting his voice rise and his chest stick out to show how proud he was.

"I had an uncle who was a medicine man; he did the same thing," said Frank. "Predicted the exact hour and date of his death . . . . The warden told him." Frank and the rest of us have a good laugh while Freddy go off and sulk 'cause we not as impressed as he think we should be.

But Freddy ain't one to be discouraged by disinterest. He come by my cabin on a sunny Saturday morning, convince me to go walking in the back country with him. He is looking for what he call badger mounds, which is places where badgers live or used to live. We was walking for an hour or so when he spot one.

"There! Right there!" shout Freddy, pointing. "A badger mound."

Looking across a bullrush-choked slough to a clearing in front of a poplar grove, I could see a mound maybe 12 feet across, breast-shaped, only three feet or so high at its top.

Freddy plunged right through the bullrushes instead of walking around; we both get our feet wet and some of that feathery cat-tail-down cling to our clothes.

"This mound's abandoned," he say, standing atop it, peering at the angled hole in the earth, where the dirt cut to look like the jutting eyebrow of a skull. "But not very long ago. A year maybe."

As he come down off the mound his foot seem to sink into the soft prairie grass. Freddy drop to his knees and pluck up handfuls of grass.

"Come here, Silas!" he yell, his voice high and excited. "Come see this. It's special. I've only found one other in all the years . . ." His voice fade away as he busy tearing grass out of what look like a deep rut maybe three inches deep and twice that in width.

"What is it?" I ask.

"It's a circle of forgiveness," he say. "This is a path I'm uncovering. When one badger did something to upset its mate, the one that had been bad would start circling the badger mound. It would circle and circle, creating a path, wearing the earth down. That badger would continue on for days, maybe weeks, just stopping occasionally to eat or sleep."

"How long did it keep that up?"

"Until its mate forgave it for whatever it done wrong."

"What if the mate wouldn't forgive?"

"Then the badger circled until it died. But none ever died. The offended mate always forgave."

Freddy was crawling along ripping grass out of the rut, which looked like the impression a tire makes when it been abandoned for a long time then lifted from where it settled into the earth.

I could see he was determined to explore the circle of forgiveness. When he got to where I was standing I had to step out of his way. As I moved aside I stepped on something in the deep grass, make me lose my balance and I almost fell. Freddy kept removing tufts of grass until the whole circle was visible, all the time repeating stories his grandfather Powder Horn had told him about badgers forgiving each other. Forgiveness among animals, he called it.

I could almost see the short-legged badger, his little claws digging into the ground at every step, his belly brushing the grass as he circled, waiting to be forgiven by his mate for whatever wrong he had done.

"You sure you could trust your grandfather?" I ask Freddy once, and he get real mad at me, run through that list of badger legends the old man taught him, as if they proved something.

What I heard about Powder Horn was that as a chief he was kind of like Chief Tom Crow-eye, the guy we is stuck with now. It said Powder Horn had a hankering to be white, and gave away Indian rights like a cowboy gives away his pay. I also heard Powder Horn have a strong liking for moonshine.

"There used to be a Badger Society," Mad Etta tell me, after I ask her about some of the stories Freddy told me. "The societies are pretty well gone now, disbanded, replaced by the Canadian Legion and the Hobbema Curling Club. Badger Society was one of the first to die out, long before I was born."

"How about the stories, are they true?"

"In those days women weren't allowed in the societies. Women weren't told the mysteries. Society members were sworn to secrecy for life. A lot of the secrets died with the last members of the societies."

"Freddy says his grandfather passed on the badger legends to him before he died. Freddy claims they're true."

"Then I guess Freddy is the only one who knows for sure," and Etta get up from her table, waddle to the stove where something evil smelling is simmering in a deep, black frying pan.

Ever since the day we found the badger mound with the circle around it, Freddy been aching to try out his theory on forgiveness. It wouldn't surprise me if Freddy, without really knowing why he was doing it, get involved with Cleo Fire just so he can do the test.

Cleo was in my class at school, was always the kind of girl who like to get a good time out of life. If you was to see Cleo sitting in a bar, she is the kind of woman you take one look at and know she be easy to take to bed.

"She have an odor about her," Frank say. He has taken her home on more than one night. "She smells like she's horny," is how Frank describe her.

I'm not sure that's true. She do like tight jeans, bright sweaters and lipstick, and she laugh and joke a lot. She is a nice friendly girl to talk to, one who, like our girlfriends Sadie and Connie, is smart enough to take her birth control pills regular, so she's got to be 22 without being tied down by a slew of kids.

"She looks like a slut," is how I heard Isobel Powderface describe her. I'm not sure if Isobel got her own tribe of kids because she is careless, or stupid, or religious.

Nobody pay much attention the first couple of times Freddy cozy up to Cleo at her table in the Alice Hotel bar. A few single guys like Gorman Carry-the-kettle and Victor Powder are a little pissed off that Freddy move in on their territory.

"Why don't that skinny little sucker go home to his wife?" Gorman say when he see Freddy and Cleo leave together at closing time for the second night in a row.

But Freddy don't go home. He stay for about ten days at the apartment in Wetaskiwin that Cleo share with Jenny Three White Loons, who work as a cashier at the Co-Op Grocery Store.

Word travel fast in a small community, plus there are always a dozen people ready to pass on bad news. Everybody is allowed a couple of mistakes, but the morning after the third night Freddy spend at Cleo's, a whole string of women come calling on Isobel Powderface, offer home-made cake and sympathy over the rotten way she being treated by her husband.

Different women have different ways of handling news like that, some figure it is their fault their husband run off so they try to do things that will make him come home, others just go wild and their friends have to keep them from going after the husband and his girlfriend with a gun. Isobel, they tell me, don't say much at all; she just get a dark look on her face, have one of her brothers change the locks on the house, pile all of Freddy's clothes, records, tools, and his guitar on the front porch of the house.

Freddy I guess figures if he going to get forgiven he might as well have a lot to be forgiven for. He gather up his stuff and go to move it into Cleo's apartment. But that's when Cleo put her foot down, say something like, "You're a nice guy to party with but I don't want an old man, especially one who just dumped his family. You better go back home while you still got the chance."

Freddy haul his stuff back home, but Isobel won't let him store it in the house even when he promise to stay outside himself. There ain't even a garage, only place he have to store his stuff is in a dog house used to belong to a real ugly German Shepherd name of Woofer who got run over by the mail truck last spring.

It is about this time that Freddy begin to circle his house.

One afternoon down at Hobbema General Store, when Freddy been jogging for close to a month, after Isobel cash her welfare check, somebody ask her how long Freddy plan to keep doing what he doing.

"I don't know or care," she say. "If the son-of-a-bitch runs around in circles long enough he'll wear the path so deep he'll be completely underground. Then I want him covered up, and I get to throw the first shovel full of dirt on his head."

I don't report that back to Freddy, but it sure don't sound to me as if Isobel is about to forgive him in the near future.

I also find out, by asking what I hope was subtle questions, that Isobel don't know the badger legends. She don't know why Freddy is running or what he expect her to do to stop him.

September first come last week along with the first frost of the season. Freddy got a month or so to get his problem solved or he going to be running in snow up to his belly button. The kids are back in school and there is nobody to watch him at all. Even the drunks don't come around after the bars close anymore.

"You believe in these stories about forgiveness among animals?" I ask Mad Etta one night when we having tea at her cabin.

"I've heard stranger things," she say. "Animals don't have wars, or booze, cars, or television, or fools who form governments. Maybe they do forgive. It wouldn't surprise me."

Yesterday I stop by to see Freddy. The circle of forgiveness is cut deep into the earth by now. There is a chill wind blowing down off the mountains. Freddy look thin, cold, and unhappy.

"Isobel don't know the badger legends," I say. "You've got to at least tell her," I add logically.

"Instinct," he reply. "Sooner or later she'll sense what it is I'm doing."

"Make it easy for yourself and help her out," I say.

"Instinct," he repeat. "She has to sense it herself. It's only a matter of time."

There is something I never told Freddy, and I don't suppose, since I've waited this long, that he'd believe me now anyway. But the day we were out at the badger mound, when I stepped out of his way and almost fell, what I stepped on was a skull, a little slant-browed skull of a badger.

Tricks

S omeday, my friend Frank Fencepost is going to get murdered because of his practical jokes. Frank he thinks everything
is funny.

"That's your trouble," I tell him one night at Hobbema Pool
Hall. "You can't tell the difference between what's funny and
what's stupid."

What make me say that is Frank been telling for about the one
hundredth time how, a couple of years ago when we was in Card-
ston for a rodeo, he fixed me up with the Big Shield twins. Frank,
when he tell the story, get so excited that if he in the bar he bounce
on his chair, make the glasses on the table slop over their edges.

I have to admit it was a good joke even if it was on me. I was
pretty excited to have a date with twin sisters. Even if it turned
out they wasn't as good looking or as willing as Frank said they
was, a date with twins would still be pretty thrilling.

"Silas never even guessed that one of the twins was a guy. I
don't know who was more surprised, Archie Big Shield or Silas."

"And Archie was the cute one," chime in Robert Coyote, who will also tease me about that evening for the rest of my life.

"Even if it was a good joke, I don't like hearing about it over and over," I grumble. "You play too many tricks," and I miss a shot I'm taking at the green ball.

"There's never too many tricks," yell Frank, take off his black, ten-gallon hat, bow and smile as if there's 10,000 people out in front of him. "Tricks make the world go round. Tricks give people something to be happy about. Tricks keep people talking. When you ain't seen somebody for a long time, first thing you do is spend time remembering the silly things you done together. You don't talk about the time you was sick, you laugh about the time you tore the culvert out of the road and somebody important drove into the hole."

"Yeah, well I for one have had enough of games and tricks," I say.

"Don't be so grouchy, Silas," somebody say to me.

"You just don't like it when the joke's on you," somebody else say.

"I'll make everybody a deal," says Frank. "Let's call this National Trick Month, whatever month it is."

"June," says Frank's girl, Connie Bigcharles.

"I'll bet," says Frank, "the Great Fencepost will bet that he can play a trick on everybody in the room, within, say, ten days."

"What if you don't?" say Robert Coyote.

"How many people is here?" and Frank walk around the pool hall, count on his fingers. There are 11, not including Frank: there are Connie, me and Sadie, Robert Coyote, Eathen Firstrider and Julie Scar, Donald Bobtail, Bedelia Coyote, Rufus Firstrider and his white girlfriend Winnie Bear, and Mad Etta sitting against the back wall on her tree-trunk chair, look like something out of an old-time movie. "If I can play a trick on each of you by the end of the month, you each got to pay me ten dollars . . . ."

"And if you don't?" says Eathen.

"Well . . ." says Frank.

"We get to kill you," growl Robert Coyote, who is about the meanest dude within a hundred miles.

Frank swallow hard until he see that Robert is joking.

"Not me," I say. "I don't want nothin' to do with it." But I get shouted down.

"Don't be a spoilsport," say Bedelia Coyote, who ain't noted for her sense of humor, especially when the joke is on her.

"Come on, Silas," say my girl Sadie. "You taking yourself too seriously these days."

"Well . . . but Frank's got to have something at stake too."

"Hey, Fencepost is invincible," say Frank, "and sometimes invisible too. If I don't play a trick on everybody in the next ten days, nobody have to pay me, especially Wetblanket Ermineskin here. If I lose I pay for everybody's pool game for a whole evening, with Frito chips and Pepsis all around."

Everybody clap their hands. There is lots of laughing and backslapping. I wonder if maybe I am growing up or something, because even though I agree to the idea, it all seem pretty childish to me.

The next day when we on our way to the Tech School in Wetaskiwin, all the guys talk about is Frank's bet. Everybody pretend to peek over their shoulder in case Frank is in view, and they check under the seat of Louis Coyote's pickup truck looking for snakes.

I keep a close eye on Frank myself. I am pretty determined he is not going to make a fool of me. But Frank is his same happy-go-lucky self. I have to admit it is fun to see him so joyful and busy.

"Well, he got me already," say Donald Bobtail, when I come back from lunch at Goldie's Café. "I took off my boots in the lunchroom, and when I went to put them on, one was full to the top with water, and Frank was rolling on the floor, laughing like a maniac."

"I figured if they was waterproof from the outside, they'd be waterproof from the inside too," yell Frank, slapping Donald on the back. "And they was."

Donald Bobtail laugh along with the joke.

I think if it had been me, I'd of made Frank drink the water. And I say so.

"Come on, Silas," says Donald, "it's only a joke."

"Yeah, you're right, it's only a joke." But I sure watch Frank careful and try to keep one eye looking behind me at all times.

The next day Frank bang off three more tricks in a row, but I stopped him from getting me. As I was walking up the hill to my cabin from Blue Quills Hall, I seen something move in the willows at the foot of the hill, and when I stare real hard I can make out Frank's shape crouched there. I still can't figure what it was he had planned, even though I sneaked back later in the day and checked over the ground where he was hiding.

When I was sure it was Frank, I scooped up a handful of gravel from the road and hucked them into the willows until Frank yell and come out with his hands up saying, "Okay, okay, you was too smart for me this time."

That evening Robert tell how Frank strung wire across the path to Robert's cabin, tripped Robert right on his face in a puddle.

"We're gonna nickname him Muddy Coyote from now on," chortle Frank, and everybody laugh lots, even Robert, who I would of figured to be mad for a year.

"I'm just gonna enjoy what happens to everybody else," says Robert. "Especially Silas. I hear Fencepost has something special for you—so special you'll be able to write one of your stories about it."

Again, everybody laugh.

"You have to catch me first," I say. "An Ermineskin can be pretty slippery when he wants to."

"Nobody gets away from Fencepost, when Fencepost puts his mind to it," crows Frank.

I tell about how I drove Frank out of the willows, and everybody boo Frank while he try to make excuses.

It was that same night, while we was having supper at Goldie's Café in Wetaskiwin, that Frank trick my girl, Sadie One-wound, though I thought again the trick might have been aimed at me. While I was gone to the washroom, Miss Goldie deliver Sadie's order of chips and gravy, spill it right down Sadie's sweater and jeans. Then Miss Goldie apologize, say that Frank paid her to do it. Connie Bigcharles was carrying some extra clothes with her and by the time I got back they already gone to the washroom to clean-up and change.

"You picked the right time to leave," grin Frank. "Sadie was second choice."

Boy, now I am on guard every second while Frank is around, and I'm even more careful when he ain't.

I wasn't there, but it was right in the Alice Hotel beer parlor that he trick Julie Scar. She is Eathen's girl and ain't been too long with our group, so Frank take it easy on her. She tossed her jean jacket on her chair, and when she come back from the restroom and sit down she find Frank put a whoopee cushion under her jacket, which make a loud, rude noise for everybody in the bar to hear.

"Everyone turned around and looked at me and I thought I'd die," say Julie, who is quiet and shy most of the time.

"Four down and seven to go," grin Frank.

"Keep your ass covered, Silas, 'cause I'm gonna get you best," and he laugh and hop from a chair to the top of one pool table, then to the second table, skipping among the snooker balls, while Eathen wave a cue at him.

Mad Etta is the next one to suffer. The joke he played on her was a classic and I bet gonna get talked about for years and years to come. Since there is electricity down at Blue Quills Hall, the Band Council have installed there two washers and two dryers, so people can do their laundry.

When Frank done it nobody knows, but he somehow got Etta's box of soap powder. The next time Etta huff down to Blue Quills with her laundry and an orange-colored box of Tide in a pillow case, Frank was lurking close by.

What Frank done was to mix fine-ground white-pine sawdust in with Etta's detergent. When she finish washing and open the machine she find her clothes speckled with millions of white dots. It take the rest of the week with her clothes hanging between two poplars at the back of her cabin, to get them part of the way back to normal.

Before Frank would agree to the bet he got Mad Etta to promise in front of all of us, that she not do him any irreparable physical damage for whatever joke he play on her.

"It was a good joke," admit Etta, smile from way down deep in her face. Her eyes twinkle like she got pen lights buried there.

As the days pass I get so I sleep lighter than ever before. I always walk looking both in front and behind me. I jump at shadows, start at every loud sound. Once I wake in the middle of the night think I hear someone on the roof. I creep out of the cabin, silent as a ghost, but I don't find nothing. Guess it was just crows walking on the shingles. Even so, next day I pound a row of nails up from under the eaves, make a nasty surprise for anybody climb on top of the cabin.

I remember old Gladys Bigcharles, who, a few years ago, got to thinking everybody on the reserve was trying to kill her. She look over her shoulder all the time, finally get so she cover her head in Reynolds Wrap, to protect herself from all the bad thoughts everyone was thinking about her.

Now, I know how old Gladys felt. Each day I get more determined Frank ain't going to get me.

"Well, he sure pulled one on us," Rufus Firstrider say that night at the pool hall.

"Did he ever," say Winnie Bear. "You're all invited for dinner tomorrow, except Frank."

Frank pound his chest and grin, raise his hands in the air like he was this Rocky guy the boxer.

What Frank done was to somehow sneak up on the turkey Rufus and Winnie keep in a pen behind their cabin. He kill the turkey, pluck it, clean it, carve his initials on its chest. Then he sneaked into their cabin and put the turkey on a plate on the table for them to find when they get up in the morning.

The more people Frank trick the more determined I become. Just in case he is after me while I sleep, I trade beds with my littlest sister Delores, though I have to pay her a dollar a night to use her bed. I also won't ride in to the Tech School with Frank anymore, and I stay clear of him both in and after class. At night, in the pool hall, at the bar of the Alice Hotel, or in Goldie's Café, I sit with my back to a corner and stay watchful at all times.

My story-writing is suffering, because I even jump when a meadowlark burble outside my cabin window, and I can't read or write but two or three lines without stopping to peer all around, make sure Frank ain't set me up for something.

There is still three days left to the end of the month when Frank trick the last person except me.

"You bastard!" Bedelia Coyote yell at Frank, outside the Tech School one morning. "I had to wash for about an hour to get clean. And I'm gonna kill you for what you done to my new blouse." She shake her fist at Frank, call him many bad names, while Frank bow from the waist just as if she was praising him.

It been raining a lot lately and the road by Bedelia's cabin is three inches deep in water. Bedelia was picking her way across that wet road. Ordinarily she could hear a car coming from half a mile away and get off the road, but Frank he hid behind a willow stand in Louis' truck, gun out onto the road when Bedelia is right in the middle. All she could do was put up her hands to protect her face from the wall of mud and water coming at her.

Even Bedelia get in the spirit after a while, and everybody laugh for about an hour over what happened to her.

Frank he save a special trick for his girl, Connie Bigcharles. I'm not sure how he accomplish this, but he put a Merle Haggard tape into Connie's purse while the two of them was in Robinson's Store in Wetaskiwin. Connie sure is surprised when the store detective grab onto her arm as she leaving. They detain her for about an hour, tell her they called the RCMP to come get her,

when Frank show up with the sales slip for the tape and they have
to let her go.

"I was gonna be mad for a year," says Connie. "I knew Frank
was behind it but I didn't know if he was gonna rescue me or not.
It was the idea of getting pinched for something I didn't steal that
really bugged me. I mean I've picked up my share of five-finger
bargains from Robinson's over the years."

"Now you see me, now you don't," laugh Frank, step out from
behind a tall spruce tree, as I walking up the hill later toward my
cabin. I jump about a foot in the air, land with my fists up to
defend myself. "Live in fear," Frank cackle, and run off through
the woods. "Be sure and look above you as well as behind you. I'm
gonna have an eagle shit on your head," he yell from deep inside
the woods.

That night I tap little stakes into the ground, string brass-colored
snare wire twice around our cabin.

The way he got Eathen Firstrider involved playing a trick on
another person as well. What I hear is that Frank got Constable
Greer, who is a nice old RCMP, to put on their computer a
description of Eathen right down to his buckskin jacket with the
beads on the back in the shape of a yellow sun rising out of a purple lake. Eathen be labeled *armed* and *dangerous*.

Then Constable Greer send Constable Bobowski, the lady
RCMP who spend most of her life giving us Indians a bad time,
down to the Alice Hotel. Soon as she arrive, Frank have Eathen
paged to the telephone.

As Eathen saunter across the bar, Constable Bobowski see him,
go into a crouch, draw her gun, tell Eathen to lie down on the
floor with his hands and legs spread wide. She search him real

careful, handcuff him and march him off to the patrol car, while about a hundred Indians stand around make rude remarks at her, then give Eathen a big round of applause as the police-car door close. But when she get Eathen to the police station, Constable Greer tell her the warrant been canceled and she have to let him go.

I am the only one left. I try to remember the kind of tricks Frank played on everybody else, stay on guard for each and every one, as well as anything else Frank's strange brain might come up with.

The final two days I stay right at home. I'm glad the cabin got only one door. I tack two gunnysacks over the big kitchen window, peer out careful, one eye at a time.

Ma sure get mad at me when she trip on the snare wire traps I laid, spill a bag of groceries in the yard. And she get even more madder when I won't go out to help her clean up.

"That's just the kind of thing he's waiting for," I say. "He's probably in one of the tall spruce behind the cabin waiting to drop something on me."

"What's *paranoid* mean?" Delores ask me that afternoon when she get home from school.

"Why?" I say.

"Because that's what my teacher said you were, after I told how you're hiding in the house scared to death."

"I'm not scared. And I'm not paranoid. I really have something to fear, Frank."

"Is he going to hurt you?"

"Not really. It's like we're playing a serious game of hide and seek. It's a contest, and I'm gonna win."

My girlfriend Sadie may never speak to me again. It wasn't really my fault; I mean I told her I'd rigged the cabin door. But Sadie forgot, and a quart of 10-30 motor oil poured on her head when she come to visit me without knocking. I haven't let her stay over for almost a week, 'cause I figure Frank will try to get me through her.

"For a guy who didn't want to do this, you sure take Frank's challenge serious," she said on a day when she was still speaking to me.

I try to explain to her that it wasn't all competition.

"It's kind of like when you know the doctor gonna prick your finger for a blood test. You don't want it to happen, even though you know the thoughts is worse than the pain."

"It's because you can't stand to have Frank get one up on you," she say. "The tricks you pull to keep from getting tricked is sillier than anything Frank does," and Sadie go home mad.

The tenth day roll around. That evening I hear Eathen Firstrider call to me from way out at the road.

"Everybody's meeting down at the pool hall," he yell.

He is careful not to get close to any of the boobytraps I laid around our cabin.

"I'll be down later," I call back to Eathen.

I know the bet don't expire until midnight, and I suspect Frank is laying for me, close by, maybe even on the roof of the cabin, or in the slough at the foot of the hill, or any of a hundred places along the trail.

About 11 o'clock I squeeze out the window at the back of the cabin. I make a long, careful circle, going at least a mile out of my way, and come into Hobbema from the highway, instead of through the reserve.

I case the back of the pool hall, peeking out of a stand of pig-weed and sting nettles, then I skulk along the side and slip in the front door. I stand with my back against the door until my eyes get used to the light. I stare around careful until I spot Frank shooting eight-ball with Eathen, Robert, and Connie.

I make a dash for a chair in the corner. I check it out careful, above, below, and behind, not even letting on that I hear all the people saying hello to me. I can't figure out what Frank got planned. He just look self-satisfied, fire a ball into a corner pocket.

I settle into that chair, lay a cue across my knees and wait. It only 15 minutes until midnight.

Frank continue to act like nothing unusual is happening; he laugh and joke with everybody. In fact lots of my friends are laughing over the tricks been played on them, tricks that sure wouldn't amuse me.

They are trying to recall the best joke ever been played on Hobbema Reserve. What always come up is Dolphus Frying Pan leading a moose to Father Alphonse's church and asking him to marry them. Everybody always been split about 50-50 as to whether it was a joke or not.

"It's been five years and Dolphus and the moose is still together," say Frank.

It is seven minutes to midnight.

My friends finally decide that the best joke ever been played was when Jean Paul Silversides and Noreen Snakeskin got married. They had a brand new Indian Affairs house to go to, and weren't planning no honeymoon, so they were about as careful as me, 'cause they expect their friends to try and play some kind of trick on them. After the wedding and reception party, they check their house over real careful and go to bed.

What they don't know is that Donald Bobtail, who study the electronics at Tech School with me, has wired their mattress so if there any moving around on the bed a big spotlight be attached to the chimney blink on and off. Well, Jean Paul and Noreen do the kind of moving around a couple supposed to do after their wedding, and by the time they finish up there is about 500 people standing outside their house in the glare of the spotlight, clapping hands in time to its blinking.

For all Frank seem to care I might as well not be here.

Midnight arrive.

"I won," I say, jumping up. "I'll just have me a Pepsi and some Frito chips now, get an early start on tomorrow night's party. We gonna cost you an arm and a leg," I say to Frank. I look around, feeling real good, expecting everybody else to be happy too.

"Hrrrmff, hrrrmff," go Frank, clear his throat. "I think there's something I forgot to tell you, Silas."

"Like what?" I say real sharp. "You mean it ain't midnight yet."

"Oh, no, it's midnight alright."

"Then what?" I sure don't like the way everybody is looking at me.

"There never was a contest," say Frank, smile like he just been freshly oiled. "It was just a few of us figured you was getting to take life too seriously."

"What do you mean there was no contest? You tricked everybody but me. I . . ."

"Did you see any of the tricks happen?" ask Frank.

I get a terrible sinking feeling in my stomach, because as I shoot every trick through my brain, playing them like a movie, I realize I only been *told* about every one. I never actually seen even one happen.

"But I ate your turkey," I say to Rufus and Winnie.

"You ate a Safeway turkey," say Rufus. "Blind Louis Coyote storing our turkey, Chief Tom, in his hen house."

"There was only one trick," say Robert Coyote, "and it was on you."

"Did you have a good time sneaking out your window and traveling two miles cross-country?" ask Sadie.

"You *were* watching me," I yell. "I knew it."

Boy, I am gonna have to live with this trick for the rest of my life. I want to be mad, but my friends are all smiling, waiting for me to smile too. They *are* my friends or they wouldn't go to this much trouble to set me straight.

I stretch my cheeks so they'll think I'm smiling, but I bet it will be a day or two before I actually do.

Graves

I t was about six o'clock on a Saturday evening when we buried Phil Cardinal right in the middle of the long, green lawn that slope from the front of his house down the hill to Jump-off-joe Creek. There was quite a crowd of people including reporters from TV, radio, and newspapers; the TV people had their bright lights set up, even though it was a clear August evening and the sun wasn't even thinking about setting.

Originally Phil wanted only his family to be present: his little son, Wallace, who is three years old, and his wife, Valerie, plus Mad Etta our medicine lady, and me, 'cause he arranged to pay me to see that nothing went wrong. But his wife wouldn't have nothing to do with the burying; her and Wallace were inside the house but I don't think they even peeked from behind the living-room drapes. When reporters knocked on the door no one answered.

It wasn't as if Phil Cardinal was dead. He is as alive as me or my friend Frank Fencepost or our girlfriends. All of us was there to see the burying, along with lots of Indians from the Ermineskin

Reserve, which is close by, and every kid from the subdivision where Phil's house is located. The kids hang around outside the rail fence on Phil's property, sort of kicking at the ground and sneaking glances our way, as if they expect to be chased away.

It kind of hard to explain who Phil Cardinal is, because there are about 20 families with that name on the reserve. He is known as Restigouche Cardinal's son, so he won't be confused with Blackie Cardinal's tribe, or One-ear Felix Cardinal's family. They is all cousins or uncles anyway, but Restigouche Cardinal sent his kids to school, and they was one of the first families to get running water and indoor plumbing when that sort of thing come available.

Phil work in Wetaskiwin where he is manager of the Co-Op Livestock Yard and Feed Mill. He studied agriculture at the University of Alberta, where he met up with and married Valerie Redwing. Valerie is so beautiful she make men breathe in sharp, just by walking into a room. She was a city Indian, a model who got her picture in the Hudson Bay Department Store ads in the *Edmonton Journal*, and her face and body was actually in the Sears mail-order catalog, in color. She was modeling blue jeans. It never occurred to me until I recognized Valerie Redwing, that people in catalogs was real.

Valerie keep modeling after the marriage, and her and Phil buy a house just off the reserve, in a new subdivision that was developed by friends of Chief Tom Crow-eye. It is called Totem Pole Estates, *the ultimate in modern living*, and it consist of 35 split-level houses built on both sides of Jump-off-joe Creek. There is also a playground, a three-hole golf course, a community center with a hot tub, a pool table and an exercise room where somebody who come down from Edmonton twice a week teach aerobics to those who want to jump around like they been bee-stung.

As far as anybody can see Phil and Valerie got everything any couple either white or Indian could want, including a real cute little boy. Wallace look so much like his daddy he could of been made with a small size cookie cutter. He is long and rangy like Phil who, I bet, could of played basketball if he'd wanted to. Wallace got long arms and he swing one of his long legs way out to the side when he walk, just the way Phil does.

I was at Mad Etta's the night Phil come to see her. He wore a business suit and white cowboy hat, park his Chrysler outside the door to Etta's cabin. I answer the door because Etta don't like to move no more than she has to. She was sitting on her tree-trunk chair against the back wall of the cabin where, in the light from the ragged wick of the coal-oil lamp, her eyes glint a kind of red. Phil is real uneasy.

"I don't suppose you know who I am?" he say.

Etta's voice come from out of the shadows, sound mysterious and scary like something Pastor Orkin, the fundamentalist fanatic, would preach about. Etta not only name Phil, she recite his family back for five generations, more than I bet he knew about. Etta she know the history of every family on the reserve, which she learn from her father, Buffalo-who-walks-like-a-man.

"Well," Phil say, "Mrs. ah . . . Black Horses, I'd like to discuss something with you . . . in private."

"Silas here is my assistant. He can hear anything either of us has got to say."

"Well . . ." Phil say again.

"Take it or leave it," say Etta.

"I'm sorry, Mrs. Black Horses," Phil say, like a school boy talking to his teacher. It sure sound odd to me to hear Etta called by her "slave name," as Bedelia would say.

To boil down what became over two hours of back and forth talk between Etta and Phil Cardinal, his problem, as he describe it, "is an ethical one." He is happy to be successful in the white man's world but he worried about leaving behind his culture and his traditions. And he is particularly worried about his son.

"Wallace isn't even going to know he's Indian until someone points it out to him," Phil say.

"How does your wife feel about this?" Etta ask.

"She's unconcerned," say Phil. "She doesn't think it important for us to remain Indian. I had to fight to buy our house here close to the reserve and not in Edmonton. She even suggested we change our name to Card, and not mention we're Indian unless somebody asks."

"What exactly do you want me to do?" asks Etta.

"I want you to listen to me. I know you understand."

Etta nod her big head up and down.

"Come back anytime," she say at the end of the evening.

Soon as his car pull away from the door, she say to me, "What do you think about him?"

"I think he's sincere," I say. "I didn't know at first—I thought he was just wanting to play Indian . . . ."

"Enjoy a little reservation chic," say Etta.

"Yeah, like Indians who wear plastic feathers when they go downtown, and buy a tape of real Indian pow-wow dancing. But I like him. What do you figure to do with him?"

"We'll wait and see. He feels real lost inside. I'll talk with him and see what he decides to do."

But Phil deciding to get buried alive sure wasn't Etta's idea. In fact he didn't tell her what he was going to do, just said he was going to do something serious.

At Etta's suggestion, Phil he hired me to watch over him once he was down under the earth, just to see that local kids or curious people didn't break off, plug up, or pour things down that vent pipe.

My friend Frank Fencepost hang around with me, spell me off when I need to go somewhere. Phil said he didn't have any idea how long he would stay buried, but he have provisions enough to last the whole six weeks of holiday what he saved up from the Co-Op Feed Mill.

His grave was a pre-cast concrete tank about eight feet long and four feet high. He stock the place with a chemical toilet, bottled water, dried food, and a sleeping bag. From the house he run an extension cord with a 100-watt bulb on the end, and thread it down the air pipe.

"Sure you don't want to take a TV, tape deck, electric blanket, maybe some Willie Nelson records?" ask Frank. But all Phil do is give him a look that could hard-boil an egg in two seconds flat.

Phil had to hire a backhoe to dig the grave, and it make a certain amount of mess steelwheeling across the big, moist lawn, before it even start with the digging. I understand Valerie was a little bent out of shape because Phil used their savings to buy the concrete tank, pay for the backhoe, and hire me for up to six weeks to keep an eye on him. Apparently they had a screaming argument in the lobby of the Toronto-Dominion Bank in Wetaskiwin the day before Phil went underground.

"We going to call you Potato Phil from now on," joke Frank. But Phil don't see anything funny about being compared to a potato.

"You know, Silas," Frank say to me, "if this guy had a sense of humor, he wouldn't have to go burying himself." I wasn't sure about that at the time, but over the weeks I think I've come to agree.

At first, all the people in the district who don't have nothing better to do, and a few who do, spend some part of every day hanging out along the southern edge of Phil's property, leaning on the white painted fence and speculating on the what, why, and wherefore of Phil burying himself in his front yard.

It get so Phil Cardinal's fence replace the sidewalk in front of Hobbema General Store as the place to hang out of a summer evening. Both kids and adults stock up on soft drinks, potato chips, chocolate bars and cigarettes, then walk down the gravel road to Totem Pole Estates, lean on Phil's fence and stare for an hour or two.

Trouble is there ain't anything quite as unexciting as staring at a four-foot length of galvanized pipe sticking up out of the earth in the middle of a lawn. The media people lose interest first, though on the third day, a lady reporter from CFCW, the country music station in Camrose, name of Elaine Crutchfield, come by and do an interview with Phil by yelling her questions down the top of the air vent, then holding her microphone over the pipe to pick up his answers.

After she set the scene for her audience she said: "The obvious question, Mr. Cardinal, is why are you doing this?"

"That would be very difficult to explain in a short time," say Phil's voice, which sound hollow and reflected back on itself, like when me and Frank were kids and played telephone by using two pork-and-bean cans tied together with string.

"Well, you'll have to admit it's unusual for someone to have themselves buried alive?"

"Yes, it is. To answer your first question, I am trying to come to terms with my fears. I felt trapped in the life I was leading. I felt as if I was already in a grave. In Indian history, if a warrior was afraid of something, say a bear or a wolf, he deliberately sought out what he was afraid of and confronted it. In my own way I'm trying to do the same thing."

"I see," say Miss Crutchfield, but it plain by the tone of her voice that she don't. "I must say you're very articulate for an . . . for a . . ."

"For an Indian," Phil cut in to say. "I have a university degree, Miss Crutchfield, do you?"

"I'm sorry," say Miss Crutchfield, who Frank when he talk to her always call Miss Crotch and then add the *field* as an after-thought. "This interview isn't live, so I'll edit all that out. But let's get back to your reasons for burying yourself. Is it death you fear, or the idea of being trapped?"

"Aren't they one and the same?"

At that point Frank whack the palm of his hand on his fore-head and roll his eyes. Frank don't have any more use for people who waste their time thinking instead of doing, than I do. He lift up the front of his *Alabama* tee-shirt to show his bare belly and say: "Excuse me, Silas, but I'm gonna stare at my belly button until it start popping out gold coins." Then he spit onto the grass under his chair.

Phil and the radio lady talk a while longer.

"Does your doing this have anything to do with your being an Indian?"

"It does."

"Would you care to elaborate?"

"I suppose it's that I feel I've missed out on something. The experience of the young warrior going out and isolating himself in the wilderness, camping in one solitary spot, waiting to dream, to catch a glimpse of his future, the animal that will be his totem, dreaming a new name for himself."

"Do you plan on taking a new name after you've spent your time underground?"

"I hope so. I want to dream like my ancestors dreamed. I want to learn the secrets of nature and humanity. Mostly I want to dream."

That interview never get broadcast. After she finish talking to Phil we walked the radio lady to her station-wagon. All the time she was packing away her recording equipment she was shaking her head.

"I was hoping this guy was a real goof," she says to me and Frank. "A fruitcake, twelve cents short of a dollar. People like to hear real weirdos rant and prattle. It makes them feel sane. But this guy's just trying to find himself and doesn't know how to go about it. Nobody cares about something like that."

"Your listeners should be interested in an Indian burying himself," say Frank. "You could pass it off as progress—white people been burying us for years—now we learn how to do it ourselves."

The radio lady smile at Frank but she don't look as if he convinced her.

Phil been buried three full days before Valerie come out of the house. All that time the drapes never been opened once, and little Wallace ain't been outside to play. A couple of Valerie's relatives drove down from Edmonton to see her, and two of Phil's brothers, one with his wife and kids along, come by. They park their cars in the driveway and try to walk to the front door without looking out over the lawn to see the grave. A few feet east of the grave is a 15-foot growth of white poplars and wild grasses separate Phil's property from the one next door. Me and Frank set up our sleeping bags there, where we have a radio and tape deck, a campfire to cook hot dogs, and our girlfriends who spend the evenings with us, even spend the night a time or two when it was warm enough and there was a breeze to keep the mosquitoes away.

For the first few days, every eight hours or so me or Frank would go to the graveyard pipe and holler down, ask if there was anything Phil needed, or wanted us to do. He always said no.

Then on the day Valerie come out of the house for the first time, he say for us not to bother him again. "I'll let you know if I need anything. I want time to dream," he say.

Valerie, when she come out of the house, do the same as her visitors, try not to look toward Phil's grave. She drag Wallace, who is dancing around and pointing out over the lawn, straight to the car. As they drive away he have his face up close to the back window staring. Valerie look drawn and tired; she wearing blue jeans and a red turtleneck sweater, both show off how beautiful she is.

She have a way of swinging her long hair, show off her neck and profile, that make my mouth water. Guess I'm not the only one.

"Oh," groan Frank, "can you imagine leaving a woman like that alone for six weeks while you bury yourself in the ground to think?"

"I can't," I have to admit.

Valerie's father, who is some kind of department manager for the post office in Edmonton, drive down on the fifth or sixth day. He is a short man in an expensive suit. I was watching over the grave alone, and he wave me away as he walk up to the pipe, in his black, city shoes, clear his throat to have a conversation with Phil.

The second week, Phil's youngest brother, Milton, come by. He is a professional cowboy, ride the rodeo circuit most of the year. He was in Phoenix, USA, when he heard about what Phil done and he fly home quick.

"Jeez, man, if you want to get away for a while, I'll take you on the circuit with me for a few weeks. It's a lot more fun than being buried. We can fly out this afternoon from Edmonton if you like. How about it?"

Phil just thank Milton for his trouble, say he'll stay put.

One of the things Phil didn't take with him, that I think he should have, was a watch.

"I don't want to be bothered by time," was the reason he gave. "My ancestors lived by the seasons, didn't have to worry about hours, or days, or even weeks."

But he *was* bothered by time.

I read in a magazine about how people who are locked up in small places, deprived of time, was what they called it, lose all track of hours and days.

On the sixth morning, which was the seventh of August, Phil called up to me: "I figure it's about the eighteenth," he said. "How close am I?"

I had to tell him it was only the seventh. He sounded real confused after I told him that. But he wouldn't let me drop my wrist-watch down to him, one that by coincidence is called a Cardinal watch, tell the date, the month, and the time down to a fifth of a second.

I sure wonder if he's used up 18 days' worth of food and drink, but I figure that's his business so I don't ask.

By the end of the second week almost everyone gone back

about their own business. Phil don't have anyone to talk to but me and whoever of my friends is keeping me company. Still he go for days without saying a word, though sometimes I think I can hear him talking to himself down there, whispering, humming, mumbling.

It was August 12th when Pastor Orkin, the fundamentalist preacher from The Three Seeds of the Spirit, Predestinarian, Bittern Lake Baptist Church show up driving a yellow school bus with the church's name hand-painted on the side, the letters all pushed together because whoever painted the sign didn't figure in advance how much room was available. There is six little kids in the bus with him, each one got a musical instrument of some kind.

The pastor come hotfooting it across the lawn, look disapproving at everything he see, strut to the air pipe and shout into it: "Woe to him that buildeth his home by unrighteousness and his chambers by wrong."

Pastor Orkin's booming voice must have scared Phil half to death.

I know both Frank and Pastor Orkin would deny that they are anything alike, but they both have a lot of nerve, venture into places nobody in his right mind would go. A couple of priests in brown dresses come by one of the first evenings Phil was underground, but they just skulked in the underbrush, fingering their beads, the setting sun flashing off the crosses at their waists.

I remember once when Phil talked about taking courses in philosophy and religion at the university, and how he wished he could have taken a lot more of those because he found them more interesting than crop rotation and animal husbandry.

"I'm glad you came by, Pastor Orkin," Phil's voice would say.

"There are a lot of things I'd like to discuss with you."

"Shalt thou reign, because thou closest thyself in cedar? Jeremiah 22:15," Pastor Orkin holler.

I want to point out that Phil has *closest* himself in concrete, but I guess that's the best Pastor Orkin can do, since they didn't have precast concrete in biblical times. It's too bad that Pastor Orkin ain't one for discussions. In his religion only the pastor talks and everyone else listen.

I am surprised though when Phil quote right back at the pastor, something about someone *which rejoice exceedingly, and are glad when they can find the grave.*

"He shall be buried with the burial of an ass," shout Pastor Orkin.

"Job said: 'O that thou wouldst hide me in the grave,'" Phil call back. "Tell me, Pastor, what comes after the grave?"

Pastor Orkin used to be a parts clerk at John Deere Tractor in Camrose before he started his own religion. He only knows things he memorized from a mail-order course on how to save souls. He look at a card he made a lot of notes on, and quote again: "But thou art cast out of thy grave like an abominable branch. Isaiah 14:19."

"'Marvel not at this,'" Phil call back, "'for the hour is coming, in the which all that are in the graves shall hear his voice': John 5:28. Don't you want to talk seriously, Pastor?"

They quote scripture back and forth but Pastor Orkin ain't smart enough to answer any of Phil's questions. The little kids get out of the bus, circle the air pipe, Pastor Orkin blow a pitch whistle and the kids play recorders and tambourines, sing "Let the Sunshine In," two or three keys away from how it supposed to be done.

The eighteenth of August do finally come around. It was along about dawn on that morning, when everything dripping with dew, that I heard the door of the house click. I had stayed alone overnight. I peek out of the poplar thicket, see Valerie on the front steps, close the door careful behind her. I crawl out of my sleeping bag and slip deep into the poplars. Valerie walk careful, as if she afraid the ground will squeak, leave black footprints behind her on the silvered lawn. She look over to where my sleeping bag is, even step one foot in the long grass, crane her neck until she sees no one is in it. She walk over to the vent pipe, put her mouth right against it, call to her husband in a whisper. I don't hear his answer, but the second thing she says is in a harsh voice, the S's sizzling.

"Asshole! How could you do this to me?" she hiss. There is a pause. "You what? You what? Well, so do I, and so does Wallace, but we don't make fools of ourselves and our family . . ."

She have a lot more to say, and I guess Phil does too, but I move off through the woods to give them privacy. Eventually I circle around and get to the truck. Valerie look my way when I start it up, but only for a second—guess she figure I got cold and went there to sleep.

It was the middle of the third week when Valerie moved out for good. Her papa and a couple of other relatives arrive first, then the Mayflower Van Lines truck, painted that same too-bright yellow as traffic signs. I'm surprised that Phil don't yell up to me to find out what going on, for the truck grunt and rumble and the storm door flap back against the house every time the movers carry out another piece of furniture.

By the end of the day the house is vacant, even the drapes is gone, and the place sure look cold. A piece of cord droop down in a sad loop, lay cockeyed across the front window pane. Valerie's papa change the locks on the doors.

Over the next few days, me and Frank and our girlfriends joke about what we'd want to take into the grave if we was planning a six-week stay.

"One thing for sure," say Frank, "Phil is proving you can't take it with you, and Valerie just proved you can."

"I'd want a TV for sure," says Connie. "And a mirror and lots of make-up to try out."

"I'd rather have a six-pack of Lethbridge Pale Ale for each day," says Frank. "A six-pack is an Indian television."

"I'd want a big stack of paper and about fifty colored pens," I say.

"I'd be afraid to be alone for that long," says Sadie.

"I'd want somebody to drop Kentucky Fried Chicken down the vent every evening," Connie add. But I agree with Sadie, what I'd really want with me is Frank, so I wouldn't be alone.

Frank grin like he just won a lottery. But what it come down to, when we get serious, is that even though it is easy for us to make fun of him, none of us would want to do what Phil is doing.

Phil's been in the dark for quite a few days now. When Valerie left forever she must have shut off the electricity at the fuse box, and the house have so many locks on it, even Frank, who claim he can melt locks by staring hard at them, ain't been able to get in. Besides, somebody who work in Wetaskiwin say Valerie arranged with Calgary Power to have the electricity cut off the same day she left.

Today, Phil's voice in the first air of daylight wake me and

Frank. The sky is low and black and I can smell the wheat ripening in the fields across Jump-off-joe Creek.

"I want to dream," Phil shout. "I want to dream!" His voice rise out of the pipe and drift off into the cold, dewy-smelling dawn.

"He ain't never gonna dream if he don't shut up and go to sleep," whisper Frank.

Coming Home to Roost

S omewhere along the way my sister Minnie has grown up without my really noticing. I find this out when, real late of a Saturday night, while I'm sittin' at the kitchen table, writing on a story, drinking coffee and thinking hard, Minnie come through the door. When I look at her I get a real shock. Instead of being a little girl with a tooth or two missing and her braids unravelled, she is all of a sudden a woman, and a pretty one at that. Her hair is blue black as a crow's wing, hang loose on her shoulders, and she filled out in all the right places. She got on bright lipstick and blue eye-shadow.

I stare at her a second and third time. I can tell by the smell of her she been drinking beer; she might even be a little unsteady on her feet.

"Hi, big brother," she say to me, flashing a big smile.

"What the hell are you doing coming home at this time of night?" I say, both louder and meaner than I intend to.

"You rather I'd stay out until morning?"

"Don't be smart. It's after two o'clock."

"Ducky Cardinal wanted to take me home with him. I could of gone."

I realize what I'm feeling is fear. As if Minnie is about to walk in front of a speeding truck. Only I don't have any idea how to pull her back.

"Ducky Cardinal's a bad dude," I say. "You don't want nothing to do with him. He's been in jail."

"Hey, lighten up, Silas. You're not my old man, and you're not a school principal, even if you act like one."

She stands with her hands on her hips, stare at me with a real surly eye, her lower lip turn out in a pout, the same one each of my sisters have. My inclination is to light into her like I was a fox and she was a chicken. I can already see the air of the room full of floating feathers. But I hold my tongue. I've seen the mistakes everyone else makes raising their kids and I've always thought I'd never be that way with my own. Minnie may be my sister and not my daughter but I still feel responsible for her.

"Sorry, sis," I finally say. "Sometimes I forget you're not nine years old anymore," and I smile over the rim of my white coffee mug.

She take her hands off her hips. I guess she was all set for a fight too. She carrying a string shoulder bag and from it she dig out a pack of cigarettes and light one up. I've seen her smoking when she walking down the hill from school with a group of her friends, but I think this is the first time she ever light up at home. She is looking at me out of the corner of her eye, daring me to say something. I consider for a while but decide not to.

"You want some coffee?" I say.

"Sure," and she get a mug off a cup-hook by the stove and I pour some for her.

"So, who are you embarrassing with your stories this time?" and she wrinkle her nose at me the way she done as a little girl. To see her do that make me remember how much I love her.

"I'm telling about the time Peter Lougheed Crow-eye was a snitch for the RCMP."

"Oh, long as you're not writing about me. I'd die if you ever wrote about me."

I take a close look at Minnie while she sitting there across the table. People you're with every day change so slowly, like a tree growing, that you never notice the small changes, only the total result.

What I see scare me a lot. To start with Minnie is pretty, even beautiful. She's wearing tight jeans with a wide, black belt, a purple blouse with all kinds of ruffles on it, and some real nice cowboy boots I bought her for her 16th birthday. As we talk about small things I realize I ain't that much older than her. I don't know how to be a father, or even if I should try to act like one to her. It's just that so many Indian girls her age go bad; the unluckiest go to the cities alone, end up drinking too much and selling themselves on the street. Others manage to get in lots of trouble at home; they get pregnant, sometimes two or three times in a row, end up living with some guy who is too young to have a family, and, when he get tired of being poor, seeing all his money go just to survive, he up and go away, and the girl and kids are left alone.

A couple of years ago I talked to Minnie about birth control. I was real embarrassed to do that and so was she. To cover her unease she make jokes while I'm talking to her. But at least she know how *not* to get pregnant. "I know I sound like a teacher or something," I told her, while I explained as best I could that a guy who'd get it on with her and not use protection is a bum, and she should run away from him like he got dollar-sized sores on his body.

But I also know that you take a healthy girl, a few beers, a car with reclining seats, a guy like Frank Fencepost, Robert Coyote, or Phil Carry-the-kettle, guys who can talk a bird out of a cat's mouth, and a girl don't stand a chance. And every time I go out to a bar with my friends, them, and sometimes me, is on the other side of the fence, hoping to score with a willing girl.

I remember Frank saying about one of his sisters, "Girls shouldn't be allowed to be teenagers until they're about twenty-five years old at least."

I try to talk to Minnie about what she going to do after she's through school. I figure if I keep talking that way it never occur to her to drop out like so many of her friends is doing right now. She's in her second half of Grade 11, and her grades are so low I don't figure she'll ever see Grade 12.

"You never went through high school," she say to me, "and you've done okay."

I have to admit she's right. "I stopped school when I was fourteen because I didn't know no better. There was nobody to tell me different. But I went back to the Tech School. I wish I had Grade 12, and I wish I'd gone to university. I was lucky to have Mr. Nichols take an interest in me. Otherwise I'd be just drifting along like most of the guys I went to school with."

"Driftin' ain't so bad, Silas. I got to party now, or life get away from me pretty soon."

I bite my tongue to keep from giving her a half-hour lecture. My stomach hurt when I think of Ducky Cardinal having his hands all over Minnie. Ducky is the kind of guy nobody want their sister to go with; he is short and squat, wear about a three-inch square belt buckle with a picture of a marijuana leaf on it. He work the rodeo circuit, and I guess is actually a pretty fair bronc rider. Good thing is that in about six weeks he'll hit the road, and if we're lucky he won't be back on the reserve until November.

I understand how Minnie thinks. I thought exactly the same way when I was 16. I'm lucky to be alive today. I just hope Minnie is as lucky.

The next day I go tell my troubles to Mad Etta. We talk for maybe an hour, drink tea from her huge blue-and-white tea pot.

"Is your mom worried about Minnie?" she begin.

"You know Ma; she's an old-time lady. She let us grow natural. She figures if half of us turn out okay she done a good job."

"But you don't agree with her."

"Etta, teenagers now got so many choices, choices that even me and Frank and my friends didn't have a few years ago."

"By the way," Etta say, making like it just an afterthought, "how did Sadie's old man, Collins One-wound, treat you after you took up with his daughter?"

"He's always been nice to me," I say. "But he's an old-time Indian. 'I got enough of my own troubles,' he said one time. 'Sadie will have to work out her own life.' "

"You figure you deserve to be treated nice?"

"I always knew I was nice," I say. And we both laugh. "But when I was sixteen I was a crime just waiting to be committed."

"Why don't you have a beer with Ducky Cardinal one night?" say Etta, "all the time remembering what you were like six or seven years ago."

"I might," I say, after a long pause.

"Ummmm," say Etta, nod her head up and down. "You found a good girlfriend to keep you in line, and you turned out better than some, and no worse than most."

If I was saying it, I would of thought I turned out a little better than *that*.

Though I am sometimes a worrier, what happened to me the next week was something totally new. I think that for three or four hours I went a little bit crazy. It was a week night and I was writing as usual. After supper Minnie said she was going down to the Hobbema Pool Hall to hang out with her friends.

"Be home by eleven," I said as she was going out. "You got school tomorrow."

Minnie didn't say a word, but she give me a look let me know how old and stupid I am. I recognize it as one I've thrown out more than a few times.

About midnight I start getting worried. By one o'clock I'm pacing around the kitchen and peering out the window every time a car turns off the highway, a dog barks, or somebody walks past the cabin on the gravel road.

My girl, Sadie, who hardly ever get mad at me, gather up her jacket and purse and head to her folks' cabin. "What's the matter with you?" she ask me. "You're acting like a worried father straight out of a movie."

Even though I know she's right, I say, "I'm worried about my sister, okay? I'm worried about who she's out with and what she's doing."

"Give her some credit, Silas. Minnie's no worse than her friends. She's got her own life. You can't look over her shoulder." Sadie bang the cabin door as she leave. Ma and the other kids are asleep.

I just don't want to see Minnie go wrong, I tell myself. If a girl can get to 18 without getting pregnant or running off to the city, or moving in with someone useless . . . .

It seem me and Minnie are almost enemies. I know that for the last few days I been coming down on her like a mean cop, and that all I have is questions, no answers.

A couple of nights before I was lecturing her about going out with a dangerous guy like Ducky Cardinal, when she look me right in the eye and say, "How old was Sadie the first time you took her to bed?"

That is what Mr. Nichols might call a rhetorical question. It don't need no answer. I can't say a word, because all I could say is, "That's different." And I guess it ain't different at all. I was 16 and Sadie was 14. Ducky is 18 and Minnie 16. It's just that when I look at Minnie she's so pretty, and *so* young.

By two o'clock, if there was anybody I could have phoned I would have, if we had a phone. I walk past Ducky Cardinal's place but the cabin is dark and his truck ain't there. I'm boiling inside. I get a feeling of panic as I imagine all the terrible things could of happened to Minnie. Then I get mad when I think that maybe she's off partying, getting drunk and having sex with some guy in the back seat of a car.

By three o'clock I know I ain't entirely rational. I hear a car turn off the highway, but I recognize its backfire as it strain up the hill; it is Louis Coyote's pickup truck. Frank Fencepost and Eustace Sixkiller went off to Camrose on business that afternoon.

But instead of stopping over by Fencepost's, the truck stop by my place. I'm already outside by the time the dust drifting past the doors. Minnie get out of the passenger side, holding a bottle of Labatt's Blue in her hand.

Frank come strutting around the truck grinning like he is happy about something.

"Where the fuck have you been?" I yell at Minnie. She is at least half-drunk, her eye-shadow smudged. She is wearing her same jeans and boots, one of my old white shirts, the tails tied in a knot on her belly. She ain't wearin' any bra and I can see her dark nipples under the thin white cloth.

"Hey, Silas, glad to see you're still up. I could sure use a coffee," say Frank, walk right past me into the cabin.

"And you look like a hooker," I yell at Minnie before she can answer my first question.

Minnie put her hands on her hips and stare mean at me.

"I'm not your kid. And it's none of your fucking business where I been, or how I look, or who I've been with." She toss her bottle into the weeds alongside the house and start to walk past me too.

I grab her arm.

"Leave go of me," and she lurch against the door jamb. "Who the fuck do you think you are, King Shit of Turd Island?"

I am so mad I can feel tears rising behind my eyes. There are so many things I want to yell, but none of them can get out of my mouth. At the same time I feel a little like laughing because Minnie's last sentence was so childish. I haven't heard anyone say that since grade school.

"Tell me where you've been," I finally yell; I've got her blocked off between the table and the stove so she can't get to the bedroom.

Frank has sat himself on a backless chair by the stove. He grin and raise his coffee cup to me.

"Hey, you know what they say, if you got the name you may as well have the game," Minnie yell back.

"If your argument's personal, just say the word," says Frank.

"You think the worst of me," yell Minnie. "So I been off turnin' tricks tonight. I fucked Frank and Ducky and Eustace, and a couple of guys I don't even remember their names. And what are you gonna do about it?" She throws the jean jacket she been carrying, into my face, and duck past me. I swing at her but just graze her shoulder. She gone behind the blanket that's the door to her and Delores' room. If you can slam a blanket behind her she does.

"Don't look at me," says Frank, still grinning. "I didn't . . . ."

"Don't talk down to me, you bastard," I scream at Frank. "I know all your filthy tricks. You screw anything that twitches . . . ."

Right then I do one of the things I am least proud of in my life. I hit my friend Frank Fencepost. Me and Frank been friends since we was babies together. Never since we growed up have we fought serious. We've always horsed around a lot, and Frank always win. Even though I'm bigger, Frank is stronger and tougher.

What was so bad about what I done was Frank wasn't expecting to get hit. I whacked him on the side of the head and knocked him off his chair. He sit on the floor next to the woodbox for a few seconds, rub his head, then it take him two tries to get to his feet, even then he have to grab onto the warming oven of our old cookstove to steady himself.

Oh, boy, I think, I am gonna get pounded good now. I get my fists ready at waist level. I ain't mad anymore. I'm not gonna try to hit Frank again. But I'm gonna defend myself.

Frank don't say a word. He just sweep his black cowboy hat off the table, cram it on his head as he goin' out the door. He don't look back as he disappear into the darkness. I think I'd of hurt less if he'd pounded me a couple of good ones.

I wait around for an hour or so in case Frank decide to come back. The sun come up but he don't. Eventually I wander over to Mad Etta's.

"Usually it people forty years old come askin' how to handle their teenagers," say Etta, after she gave me a strong cup of coffee.

"I didn't ask to be the *man* in our house. It just worked out that way."

"Has Minnie ever been in trouble?"

"No. Minnie's not a bad girl. It's just that she's so young to have to make choices."

"So you'd like her to be safe, and sober, and smart, and for her friends to be the same way."

"No," I say, but I drag the word out for three or four seconds 'cause I'm thinking about it.

"You'd be happier if she stayed home and read books, and if she went to a craft class at Blue Quills Hall on Saturday night."

I don't even answer that because I know it's silly. But it's also true.

"You ain't one bit different from other parents," Etta go on. "Seem to me I remember you pulled a deal to help Julie Dodging-horse run off with her boyfriend a couple of years ago."

I nod that I did. I wonder how Etta come to know about that?

"How'd you feel if some guy helped Minnie run off with Ducky Cardinal?"

"I'd kill him," I say. "Ducky Cardinal's a bum."

"Ummmm," say Etta.

There is a saying about your chickens coming home to roost. I don't like that feeling at all.

"Silas, I'm gonna tell you what you don't want to hear. First of all you got to give Minnie credit for being the bright young woman you've helped make her. When Illianna was her age she'd already gone off to Calgary and was on her own. She didn't have anybody behind her pushing her along, or anybody watching over her . . . ."

"But everything's more dangerous now. There are more guys like Ducky Cardinal. There are more drugs. The streets in the city are meaner."

"Silas," say Etta, and she come and put her big arm around my shoulder. "You'd never admit it even to yourself, but you're a little jealous of Minnie and her friends."

"Never."

"Whatever. But the thing you got to remember is, if you don't let her go you'll lose her altogether." Etta guide me toward the door. I think she doled out all the advice I going to get, at least today. But she surprise me by following me outside.

"Silas, I want to walk you down to the bush behind my cabin here, show you something."

It is April and the trees are still bare, but covered in swollen-up buds. We kick last year's soggy leaves as we walk maybe a hundred yards into the poplars behind Etta's cabin.

"You probably don't remember, Silas, but there was a well down here. Stopped using it over twenty years ago. My old man was still living then; he built a fence around the well so's kids or animals wouldn't fall in. The casing rotted and the well caved in years ago, so the place is safe, but some of the fence is still standing. It's the fence I want you to look at."

What I see in front of me is a strange sight: a fencepost wired to a tree. The bottom of the fencepost is about four feet off the ground. What I guess happen is when Etta's husband build the fence, he wire a little sapling to the fencepost. Over 20 or more years that tree growed way up, got bigger around, and pulled the fencepost out of the earth, carry it up in the air until it hanging useless.

"Well," says Etta, "what do you see?"

"A tree pulled a fencepost out of the ground," I say. "Does it have something to do with Frank?" I ask.

"No," she say, real cross. "It don't have a damn thing in the world to do with Frank. I didn't think you were so stupid, Silas."

"Sorry," I say.

"That fencepost was part of a gate. Only my husband, Lawrence, closed up the gate. The circle of wire was part of the gate. That little sapling grew up through the wire circle, over the years it got bigger and bigger, until it pulled the post up and out. But you don't pay close enough attention. See what the wire's done to the tree."

Sure enough, the wire has cut almost clean through the tree; the tree is going to be cut in half in maybe just one more year.

"The young tree and the post stayed too close together," Etta go on. "Now neither of them is good for anything. Do I have to take a picture of this scene and have you carry it around in your pocket before you catch on to what I'm saying?"

"No," I say, after a long pause. "I catch on. But it ain't gonna be easy. I don't want to cut those wires."

"Silas, you're usually smarter than this. Look, I've seen you take your little brothers and sisters out sliding on the long hill by your place. You bundle the kids up good, put them on the sleigh, push them down the hill—once you let them go, ain't a damn thing in the world you can do but hope the sleigh goes straight, don't tip over or hit no trees."

"You make a good point," I say. I don't tell Etta, but what I always wanted was to sit on the front of that sled and steer.

I don't sleep at all. Come morning, instead of ride to Wetaskiwin to Tech School with Frank, Rufus Firstrider and Donald Bobtail the way I usually do, I get out on the highway at seven o'clock hitch a ride with a school teacher driving up from Ponoka. I sit in a different part of the classroom from my friends, don't even look at the spot where I guess Frank is sitting.

I would of felt a lot better if at least part of what I accused Minnie of was true. But it wasn't. Turn out her and Ducky was visiting some married friends of theirs in Wetaskiwin, have a couple of beers and play cards until midnight. On the way home Ducky's truck broke down, and a while later Frank and Eustace come along in Louis' pickup. They work on the truck for a while, then Eustace, who is a pretty good mechanic, say he'll stay and finish up with Ducky, while Frank drive Minnie home.

Boy, do I have some apologies to do.

It is easier to make up with Sadie. I spend the next two nights at her place so I don't have to face Minnie. I hate to feel this way, tense as if my ribs was taped; it mean I can't concentrate on my writing or much of anything.

I figure the worst thing Frank can do is punch me out good. If we're even, he won't have reason to be mad at me anymore.

On the third day at lunch at Tech School I walk up to Frank where he leaning on the sunny side of the building having a cigarette.

"I was wrong," I say. "I'm sorry I hit you. I haven't got enough friends I can afford to lose one."

Frank he grin out of his missing-toothed mouth.

"Hey, you got a left almost as good as Connie's. If I'd seen it coming I'd of flexed my ear and broke your hand."

I apologize for a while more and Frank joke some more. I am sure happy to be his friend again.

I feel so good I cut class that afternoon and head back to the reserve in Louis' truck. I'm parked outside the Reserve School when it let out for the day. Minnie and about five of her friends come laughing down the road. I beep the horn a couple of times, lean across and open the passenger door.

Minnie scowl at me.

"What do you want?"

"I come to apologize. Get in."

"So let's hear it." She sit on the outside edge of the seat.

"It's not near as hard to say you're sorry when you know you were wrong. I *am* sorry, Minnie. I know you're not a bad person. I was way out of line the other night."

"Everybody's entitled to get crazy once in a while," she say, close up the truck door.

"I'll try not to be so hard on you." I let the truck coast down the hill, turn it onto the side road to our cabin.

"You expect too much from me. I'm not smart like you and Illianna, or even Delores. I don't like disappointing you all the time. But I'm not a baby."

"I know that. But life was a lot easier when you were a little girl." We get out of the truck and go inside. I put on the kettle to make coffee.

"Do you remember when Pa left us for good?" Minnie nod her head. "You said you wanted me to be your father. And I said I'd always be around if you needed me . . . ."

"And you have been."

"I guess I just don't want to let you go yet."

I pour hot water into the coffee mugs. Minnie get the Carnation milk off the counter.

"We can be close, Silas. Just don't hold on so tight. You want to make my decisions for me, clothes, school, friends . . . ."

"I feel responsible for you."

"Silas, I don't need a father, or a brother," and she pause for almost too long. "What I need is a friend. One that don't give orders or make judgments. One who accept me for what I am . . . . You do that with all *your* friends, why can't you do it for me?"

"But I see all the mistakes you could make."

"Let me make my own, Silas."

"Minnie, I've been down the road ahead of you; I just want to show you where the potholes are."

"It's okay to show me; just don't try to carry me."

I smile at that. I'm just about to step around the table to hug her. But before I can everything come crashing down.

"That's why you got to understand about me and Ducky," she go on. "I'm goin' on the rodeo circuit with him. He bought a camper to fit on his pickup. We take off for the States end of next week."

"No," I shout.

"I thought you agreed to loosen up your grip."

"You're not going on the rodeo circuit. Ducky Cardinal's nothing but a . . ." And even though I know it is about the worst thing I can do, I yell on and on, until Minnie stand up to my face and say some awful things back to me. She slam out of the cabin, promise as she leave that she gone for good.

"So go!" I yell. But there is only the thud of the shut door to hear me. I am as much mad at myself as I am at Minnie.

I pick up my heavy, white coffee mug and throw it against the far wall. It don't even got the decency to break; it just bounce off the wall, lay in the corner next to the stove, staring at me like an all-knowing eye.

The Sundog
Society

"**I** don't have to defend myself to no one," William Two Young Men shout into my face. He got a hold of the front of my shirt and his nose is about two inches from mine. "I'm only gonna tell you this once, so you never make a mistake like you just did again." He got me pushed up against the door of Blue Quills Hall. All I done was say to my girlfriend, Sadie One-wound, that I heard the story many times of how William Two Young Men cheated Moab David, but I said it too loud and William overhear me.

"You come here and listen too," he say to Ruth Two Young Men, who until about five minutes ago was Ruth David. He loosen some the grip that he got on me. Ruth wearing her bride dress and she hang on to the arm of her new man, William's son, Grafton Two Young Men.

"Forty years ago," William say to us, "Moab David and me start up a lumber business with nothing but two axes and a pony to skid out the logs. We work hard and make a pretty good start. I deposit my share of the money in the bank to use for more equipment and to hire men to work for us. Moab David, he deposit his money too, in the Alberta Government Liquor Store and the Alice Hotel beer parlor. I try to talk to him, but he just don't give a care about the business. All the equipment was bought with my money," and he wave his big brown finger right under my nose when he say that. William Two Young Men have a square jaw and a head full of hair the color of melting snow. His brown eyes is clear and he hold his shoulders straight.

"Finally, I suggest to him that we split up. Your papa," he say staring straight at Ruth, "come out of it with his ax and his wages; that was all he had owing to him." William stop and take a deep breath of the cold air. "That is the truth of what happen and I don't want to hear about it no more." He turn away from me and the wedding party, head down the steps of the hall.

That sure ain't the way the story been told when I heard it, but then I always heard it from Moab David.

That business at the wedding happen to me about a year ago now. Tonight, as usual, old Moab David is drunk. I spot him weaving across the Alice Hotel beer parlor toward the table where I'm sitting with my friend Frank Fencepost.

"Your ears good and empty, Silas?" Frank say to me. "If they ain't, you better clean them out 'cause Moab sure to fill them full."

Frank is right. Moab David is one of them old men who got only one story to tell, but he spend the whole rest of his life telling it over and over.

I always wonder where guys like Moab David get money. He ain't worked in years yet he always seem to have change to buy a beer. He sleep most nights at the Salvation Army what occupy the basement of a dark brick building over behind the Saan Department Stores. The door to the shelter painted a boxcar red, and as soon as you open it you get hit in the face by a Lysol smell. The basement floor painted a slippery gray and there is a dozen or so roll-away cots scattered about the big room. Me and Frank slept there one night when Louis Coyote's truck wouldn't start on account of the cold.

Salvation Army in Wetaskiwin is run by a Brigadier Birkland, a man about 35, who wear a blue uniform and a wine-and-blue cap that too big for his head. His skin is a pale yellow color. He got warts on his face and flat orange eyes like a chicken. But he got a good heart and I've heard that on nights when Moab David stay too long at the bar, Brigadier Birkland open up the door to the shelter and bring Moab in from where he sleep like a dog curled up in the doorway.

I'm not sure if Moab David know Frank and me by name or not, but he settle in to our table as if he do. He smile a lot and pass the time of day real friendly, but he have a kind of authority about him, and it seem, at least to a couple of young guys like us, that it wouldn't be polite to tell him to get lost.

We know we going to hear the story of how him and William Two Young Men start off in business together a long time ago, get timber leases from the Government, cut, saw, and sell lumber. But then something happen and they don't be partners no more. Moab be back on the reserve not do much of anything, while Two Man Lumber Ltd. grow into a real big company.

When Moab get started on the beer I buy him, he don't disappoint us. I've heard the story so many times I can almost move my lips along with him. When I was a kid he used to come by our cabin and tell the same story to Ma and Papa. He would talk to me and my sister Illianna too, tell us not only his sad story, but others about when he was young and used to belong to the Sundog Society.

The young men of Indian tribes used to form kind of exclusive clubs that they called societies. In real old days, they compete with each other to see who could act the bravest, take the most scalps, steal the most horses and women from enemy tribes.

"We'd go out on raiding parties," Moab would tell me and my sister, "usually just against other bands from this reserve. Us Ermineskin Indians we'd go raid the horses of the Louis Bull Band, or the Dakotas. One time we went as far west as Duffield, stole from the Stony Indians I bet fifty horses," and Moab would chuckle and tell how they'd crawl on their bellies through the grass, sometimes sneak right into the other Indians' camp to steal furs and supplies.

"I was what was called a Worthy Man," Moab go on, " 'cause one time I creep all alone right into the *tipi* of a Stony Chief, take his blanket and medicine bundle. In the real old days I would have had to take his scalp too, but when I was young we don't kill like that no more.

"Our society would do dances at the pow-wows too," say Moab, "we'd dress up in feathers and beads, put mean warpaint on our faces, sometimes dance for a whole day at a time."

Moab David's society pick the name Sundog, he say, because of the magic reflections that sit in the sky on one or the other side of the sun when the weather is terrific cold. I read in the dictionary up at the Tech School that there have to be ice crystals in the air for a sundog to take shape. It sure strange that something so fiery depend for its life on ice.

Moab tell us kids stories for hours and hours at a time, and boy, I sure do figure Moab David was at one time an important Indian. I bet that if he'd lived a hundred years ago he would of been a chief. Moab don't say so outright, but it pretty plain he think so too.

"It is Indians who learn and take on white-man ways that break up our lives more than white men," he say. "White people ain't interested in us. Give them the chance and they'll mostly leave us alone. It's Indians who want to be white that hurt all of us," and that start him off on the story of how he was cheated by William Two Young Men. My folks would nod their heads in all the right places, and I remember thinking how sad it was that a brave man like Moab David have his life turn out so awful.

"And he take my woman too," Moab David would yell, bang his fist on the kitchen table in our cabin, make the teacups bounce. Moab claim he and Bertha Monoose was promised to each other, but after he lose his business she leave him for William Two Young Men.

"All them horses I stole from the Stonys, I give them to Bertha's father like a brave supposed to in those days, and her father promise Bertha would be my woman when I was ready for her."

Back at the Alice Hotel bar Moab is repeating his story. "One day William and his lawyer got me to sign a paper. I don't read so I put my X where they tell me, like I done lots of times before. But that time was the last. They tell me I signed away my share of our business. William say I can stay around if I want, work for him for wages. Can you imagine me doing that after I owned the company?"

He slam his fist on the table, make the change and beer glasses jump in the air.

I'd guess Moab to be 60 years old. He must have been pretty good looking as a young man, but now he got a bad strawberry for a nose and a face like red cabbage. He is short and stocky, stooped some in the shoulders, but his eyes bright as a weasel's in a trap, and they look out of his face with about as much hate.

I watch him close and finally figure out how he always manage to have beer money. When he come to sit with us he put down in front of him 40 cents for a beer. Then he drink one of ours. We order another round and while the waiter is putting down the beer and picking up money Moab drag his 40 cents over the edge of the table into his hand. After the waiter is gone he drop the money back on the table, nod his head to indicate it pay for his next beer.

"After I had the business stole from me I went on a good drunk for two weeks," he say. "Bet you'd of done the same thing if you was cheated. I should have took my gun and evened things up right then," and he bang his fist on the table again.

Then he retell the story of how Bertha Monoose go off and marry William Two Young Men. He actually get tears in his eyes and hit his hand on the table so hard a glass of beer tip over on the green towel tablecloth.

I remember how Ma say she never remember Moab having anything to do with Bertha Monoose. But if Moab say it, it must have been so.

I don't call him on the business about the money. Me and Frank just got our unemployment checks, and, no matter how you look at it, Moab ain't had a good life. So I guess we can afford to buy him a beer or two. He must have been 40 years old before he married to a lady who died and left him with a baby girl named Ruth just a couple of years older than me, who been raised up mainly by a couple of Moab's sisters.

Mr. Nichols, my English teacher and principal down to the Tech School in Wetaskiwin, when I told him that Grafton Two Young Men and Ruth David was getting married, said, "That reminds me of the story of Romeo and Juliet."

I read about Romeo and Juliet because Mr. Nichols say I should, but it got too many *thous* and *thees* in it; it difficult for me as if it been wrote by a white lawyer. I seen the show though, directed by a man from Italy whose name start with Z. The movie was sad enough to make me cry, and I guess if you stretch things a little, William and Moab could be the fathers in that story.

"But, by God, I get some of my own back," Moab say to me and Frank. "You know last year when my Ruth marry with Grafton Two Young Men?" I nod to show that I know. "I wasn't even invited to the wedding, did you know that?" I nod again.

"Well, sir, I went out there anyway. Walked right up to them as they was coming out of the ceremony. I speak to William in Cree 'cause I know he don't like to talk in the old language no more. I say to William Two Young Men, 'I want some of what's coming to me.' And that bastard, you know what he say to me? He say, 'You coming to sell your daughter, Moab?' But I stand right there and stare him down.

" 'How much do you want?' he finally ask.

" 'A thousand dollars,' I tell him. 'I give my word I never ask for more, 'cause a thousand dollars is a lot of money to a poor old man like me,' I say. 'And about all I got left to give in this world is my word. You took everything else that belong to me.'

"I just keep staring him down. Well, you should of seen his

face. He get all excited because I'm making him look bad in front of his rich friends.

"'I think you deserve that much, Moab,' he say to me, and he reach into the pocket of his fancy white suit, bring out his check book and lean it up against the door of Blue Quills Hall while everybody stand around in the cold. Then he write to me, Moab David, a check not for a thousand dollars, but for five thousand."

Both me and Frank make faces to show we is really impressed.

"What did . . . ?" Frank start to ask, but Moab interrupt him.

"You know what I done with the money?" Moab smile and slap his hand, palm open, on the table again. "I got it all in the bank. I go over to the Bank of Nova Scotia in Wetaskiwin and I tell them, 'Hey, I got a lot of money here and I want to sign it up in an account, one that I can't touch, to go to the first grandchild of Moab David,' and boy, for a few minutes those bankers treat this old Indian like he was really somebody.

"I been to see Ruth a few times since she married," he go on, "and she cry some when I tell her what I done with that money she seen William give to me, and she don't think so many bad thoughts about her old papa no more."

Moab smile at us with his sharp brown eyes, take a drink from his beer, reach across the table take a cigarette from my package. Then he stand up and wander off toward the toilets, weaving a little like he walk into a strong wind.

"Boy, it must hurt him to tell a story like that," say Frank.

"I think it really do," I say, but I am already remembering the day of the wedding.

What Moab don't have no way of knowing is that his daughter Ruth and my girl, Sadie One-wound, is friends. Sadie was one of the bridesmaids that day, and because she was there I got invited too. There was six bridesmaids and Sadie was the one walk at the far end of the line, so I guess her and Ruth wasn't that good a friends. Sadie wear a salmon-colored dress of slippery material, and have some yellow roses pinned to her chest. Moab don't have any idea that I was there when him and William face each other down.

It was cold on the day of the wedding. There was a single sundog off to the north side of the sun, pale yellow as an orange in a bowl of milk. Everything covered in white frost, thick as whiskers. Most of the sky was white too, and come down real close and wrap everything up; it seem even to come right into the Blue Quills Hall, which today being used like a church. Off in the distance there is cloud on top of cloud, black on top of white, look like thunderheads boiling around, except we all know there ain't thunderstorms in February.

A preacher come all the way from Calgary to do the marriage service, some say it is because William Two Young Men donate so much money to his church, one called Alliance Pentecostal. The reverend have a face like a bowlful of apples and say lots of "Praise the Lord," and "Praise Jesus," before he get around to the actual wedding.

Ruth David wearing a long white bride dress and Grafton is in a white jacket they say cost over $50 to rent from a store in Edmonton. When the reverend ask "Who gives this woman?" Chief Tom Crow-eye say, "I do," in a voice loud enough to wake up anyone who might have dozed off. He too have on a white jacket and got his hair combed up to a peak in the front.

Chief Tom's girlfriend, Samantha Yellowknees, was with him. The Chief stare all around with his beady little eyes, trying I bet to figure how he can get invited to "say a few words" to the con-gregation. I hear he been asked to give a toast to the bride at the reception party later. "I bet it be more like a whole loaf than just one toast," is what Frank have to say about that. Chief Tom can talk for an hour without stopping, and he don't even have to be asked a question to get him started.

It was as we coming out the doors of Blue Quills Hall after the ceremony that I spot, in the distance, Moab David walking up the hill toward us. He taking long steps and kick a leg out to one side as he walk. He must of mooched a ride down from Wetaskiwin, as I sure don't figure him to walk the whole 11 miles. He wearing a red-and-white checkered mackinaw, old khaki pants and work boots. His head was bare.

The married couple was in a hurry to get in the wedding car which warmed up and waiting by the side of the hall. It was a new Chrysler New Yorker, their wedding present from William Two Young Men.

As Moab David get closer, he staggered to one side as if some-body put a hand on his shoulder and give him a good push. Every-body just stand and stare at everybody else until he reach the bottom of the stairs.

"Hello, Papa," Ruth said to him, but he hardly look at her. He stare up at William and Bertha.

"I want some of what is coming to me," Moab David say in a voice a lot louder than he need to use. His voice thick with drink and the white part of his eyes look red as a dog's.

"You come to sell your daughter, Moab?" William Two Young Men say as he walk forward to the head of the stairs. "How much do you want?"

"A thousand dollars," say Moab David, stick out his chin and chest like he is looking for a fight.

William Two Young Men reach into the inside pocket of his suit and take out a shiny brown wallet. He open it and look inside. I'm near to him and see that there are lots of red 50's, but he take out a $20 bill and put the wallet back. He fold the bill three times and toss it so it lands on the packed snow a couple of feet in front of the bottom step.

"That's all you'll get, and it's more than you're worth," say William Two Young Men.

I whisper to Sadie that I hear the story many times of how William cheated Moab out of his interest in the lumber business they started when they was young. Soon as I say it I can tell my voice carried, and I see by the mean look on William's face that I'm in trouble. But at that moment he still staring down at Ruth's father.

Moab David glared all around, like maybe he wish he had some friends to help him out. The $20 bill was unfolding itself on the snow, twisting slow, like maybe it was a worm don't like being on the cold ground.

The weather seem to have got warmer as the black clouds move closer and darken the white sky. The sun still glowed through a white haze, but the sundog was gone. Moab's boots chirped on the packed snow as he move forward. He slip a little as he bend and grab the bill up into his hand. Then he turned and walked away as fast as he was able, kind of sideways at first, like a dog afraid he gonna get kicked.

The Election

"Chief Tom been elected by acclamation for the last four terms," say Bedelia Coyote. "I, for one, think it's time we did something about it."

"Who is this guy Acclamation who cast all the votes for Chief Tom?" ask my friend Frank Fencepost. "I bet he's just like Chief Tom and don't even live on the reserve. At least I never met him if he does."

"Be serious," say Bedelia.

Being serious is what Bedelia is best at. Frank describe her as a feminist, conservationist, anti-nuclear trouble-maker. And that's on a day when he ain't mad at her. But we have to admit Bedelia been a permanent thorn in Chief Tom's side for quite a few years.

"If we run a strong candidate, we stand a chance of beating Chief Tom. He's forgot how to fight an election."

"Baptiste Sixkiller is the strongest guy on the reserve," say Frank. "I seen him lift the back wheels of a Fargo pickup truck two feet off the ground, and there was ten guys in the truck box."

"Baptiste also has an I.Q. the same size as his hard hat," snap Bedelia.

Chief Tom Crow-eye ain't done nothing but line his own pockets, and the pockets of a few friends, all at reserve expense. And the pockets he's lined with mink belong to his girlfriend, Samantha Yellowknees. Chief Tom left his wife a few years ago, and him and Samantha live in a highrise apartment in Wetaski-win. Samantha is an Eastern Indian, a Huron somebody say, come out here from Ontario to be the brains behind Chief Tom, who would still be cutting brush for the CNR if Samantha hadn't showed up.

"Alright, alright, my friends," says Frank. "Hold the applause, please. I agree to be your candidate. After all who would make a better chief than me?"

"Don't make us answer that," we say, frowning. When we feeling happy, we joke that Frank would make a great politician because we know right from the start that he is lazy, incompetent, and dishonest.

"I've got one indispensable quality," Frank grin.

"And what could that be?" we ask.

"I been to bed with over half the women under thirty on this here reserve, and a few over thirty too. That the best preparation for political office I know of, if you're a politician you spend *all* your time screwing people."

We have to agree that's true, but we still don't want Frank for our chief. What we do is try to talk Bedelia into running. But she won't.

"We want to be certain to win," she say. "I don't think the people of Hobbema are ready for a radical leader just yet."

Nothing we can do will change her mind. So we have to search out a candidate.

"Be serious," say Bedelia. "Last guy to run against Chief Tom was Rider Stonechild. For every vote he got, Chief Tom got five."

"If you ain't gonna do the obvious and nominate me," says Frank, "then how about Mad Etta?"

"I agree," I chime in. "There ain't nobody wiser, or kinder, or . . ."

"Larger!" yell Frank.

". . . and she can be tough when she has to be," I go on.

"People wouldn't go for it," argue Bedelia. "We know Etta is best but she wouldn't fit the image of a chief. Plus, much as we hate to admit it, Etta is old. We need somebody who is smart, young, and look good too. Somebody tough but not greedy, who can't be bought off by white men or crooked Indians."

"Father Lacombe is dead," I say.

"And Wayne Gretzky is too busy," says Frank.

After arguing among ourselves for about three hours we finally decide to approach Victor Ear. Victor look too much like a used-car salesman to suit me, but he do have the qualifications we is looking for. He live on the reserve, is engaged to a pretty girl name of Philomena Bluewater who is training to be a nurse. He been to a community college in Edmonton, have a diploma in business management, earn his living keeping books for a big construction company in Ponoka. Vic is not quite 30, but he can speak real good in public, belong to the Ponoka Lions Club, work for the United Way campaign and belong to something called Toastmasters, sound like an advanced cooking class for bachelors which Victor is.

"Chief Tom *can* be beaten," we tell Vic, when we call on him at his house. "People are sick and tired of Chief Tom, they just don't know it yet. Name one thing he's ever done for us?"

Vic and the rest of us are silent.

"Tom Crow-eye don't even live on the reserve. Him and Samantha travel all over the world at our expense. All they've ever done was find cushy jobs for a few of their friends."

"*We're* all gonna expect cushy jobs if *you* get elected," Frank say.

"No we're not," shout Bedelia. "We want an honest chief."

"Okay," say Frank. "Just one cushy job, for me."

Victor take a day to think over our proposition, talk about it with his fiancée, before he say yes.

Right after Victor submit his papers, we ask the Hobbema Chapter of the Ermineskin Warrior Society to throw a dance at Blue Quills Hall raise money for the campaign.

It is by the turnout at that dance we know how many people agree with us that Chief Tom need replacing.

"Everybody and their tomcat is here," Frank yell above the music. We charged everybody five dollars to get in. Ben Stonebreaker donated a couple of cases of soft drinks and Frank liberated another couple of cases from a Dominion Bottling truck in Wetaskiwin. An Indian musical band called Wounded Knee pound out country rock and everybody have a happy time.

With the money we made, Bedelia arrange to have posters printed; they have black letters on fluorescent pink paper, say VOTE VICTOR EAR FOR CHIEF. Me and Frank and about two dozen other people paper abandoned buildings in town with posters, tack them to trees and telephone poles, tape them to abandoned car bodies, and anything else that ain't liable to walk off.

By the time Samantha arrange to get posters done for Chief Tom, almost every space in Hobbema been plastered. Besides his posters is covered in big paragraphs of fine print, tell in too many words, just like Chief Tom himself, all that he accomplished for us Hobbema Indians in the last few years.

People on the reserve ain't noted for going to political meetings, but at the very first candidates meeting at Blue Quills Hall about a hundred people turn out and they all come to hear Victor. Each candidate get ten minutes to talk. Victor finish in seven. But by the end of ten minutes Chief Tom ain't even warmed up yet, and Rider Stonechild, who chair the meeting, have to ding a bell about ten times to get the chief to shut up. Victor got cheered long and loud. When Chief Tom try to keep on talking, people boo until he sit down.

As everyone filing out we can hear Samantha Yellowknees yelling at Chief Tom.

"I wrote you a ten-minute speech and you never got past the introduction. You rambled like an idiot. This isn't the legislature, you have to be brief and pretend to be intelligent." Samantha stomp her foot hard and walk away from the chief, scribbling notes on the clipboard she always carry. We all thankful that Samantha ain't an Ermineskin Indian or she'd run for office herself and we'd have a really hard time beating her.

"Trouble in paradise," say Bedelia, laughing behind her hand.

Victor Ear set up his campaign office in what used to be a hot-dog stand next to Fred Crier's Texaco Garage. When she can get time off from the hospital, Philomena Bluewater help out at that office. We have so many people interested it hard to find something for everybody to do.

"Hey, this easier than I ever expected," say Victor. "Everybody I meet tell me they going to vote me in," and he smile his nice, friendly smile.

The campaign couldn't be going better. That is until one Saturday morning we walk into the office right after breakfast and find Samantha Yellowknees sitting across the desk from Victor Ear.

"What are you doing here?" demand Bedelia.

"Just visiting," say Samantha, who is wearing a raspberry colored dress with white trimming, have her hair pulled into a tight bun. "Just because Victor and Tom differ on political matters doesn't mean we can't all be friends."

"Maybe after Victor is elected we'll be friends with Tom again," say Bedelia, "but until then you're not welcome here."

"Don't be so unfriendly," say Samantha. "Victor doesn't mind conspiring with the enemy, do you Victor?"

"Samantha doesn't mean any harm," Victor say, but he have kind of a guilty look about him when he say it.

"Samantha always mean harm," snaps Bedelia. Then to Samantha she say, "You know we don't have anything against Tom Crow-eye personally. Most of us can remember back to when he was a nice guy. It's you we're after, Samantha, and it's you we're gonna get."

"Have it your way," say Samantha, smile nice at everybody and walk out.

"What did she want?" Bedelia ask Victor.

"Like she said, she was just visiting," Victor say back. "Weren't you pretty hard on her?"

"You don't know her like we do," say Bedelia.

By this time, it look like Chief Tom pretty well given up. He ain't campaigning much at all. Unless something bad happens, Victor Ear going to be our next chief.

That's why it surprise me a lot when a couple of days later

Victor suggest me and him go for a walk 'cause he have something serious to talk about.

"I think you're the one who's likely to understand what I have to say, Silas. You're a smart fellow." Victor put an arm around my shoulder when he say that, have to reach up to do it. "I've spent the last two evenings discussing the political situation here on the reserve and in the Alberta Indian Community in general with Samantha Yellowknees. She's made some very telling points, mainly that none of us, especially me, has any political experience. What Samantha says we need, not only in the campaign, but after the election, is somebody with real political know-how."

"Somebody like Samantha?" I say.

"Right. And I think she would be an asset to my campaign team. The problem is I don't know how to tell Bedelia and the others."

"And you think I can help."

"You're not as radical as Bedelia. I mean she does get pretty pushy at times. And you seem to be able to keep your boisterous friend Frank Picketfence under control."

"Posthole," I correct him.

"Yeah, him. Listen, Samantha promise she can bring all her and Tom Crow-eye's friends over to our side too. That way we won't have to be enemies, and Samantha can teach me the ins and outs of political fighting. Her experience will be invaluable."

"But if you work with Samantha nothing will have changed. She'll just have a new puppet to pull the strings on."

"Believe me, Silas, I'm my own man."

"Then why not prove it by going it alone? Without Samantha and her friends you could really do some good for our people."

"Silas, in politics things never change." Victor spread his hands wide, palms open to show he going to explain something important. "If you were a hockey player who would you rather play for, the Edmonton Oilers or the Hobbema Wagonburners?"

"That's easy," I say. "The Oilers are champions and get paid a bundle; Hobbema Wagonburners are just a pickup team."

"Case closed," say Vic.

It sure didn't take Victor Ear long to become a politician. Or for Samantha Yellowknees to abandon a sinking ship. But Samantha she just take a short swim from one ship to another. We now see Samantha and Victor and Chief Tom's sneaky friends having dinner at the Travelodge Restaurant in Wetaskiwin, and I bet, putting the bills on an Ermineskin Band credit card.

Then one evening Samantha's little red sports car spend the night in Victor Ear's driveway. Philomena Bluewater go around with a permanent scowl on her face, and when somebody (Frank Fencepost) have the bad taste to ask, she say her engagement to Victor is off.

We can only imagine how bad Chief Tom is feeling. To add to his troubles Premier Lougheed went and retired, and some other guy who used to play football for the Edmonton Eskimos is now Premier of Alberta. The rumor is that the new premier going to sweep out the deadwood among his MLAs and there ain't no deader wood than Chief Tom. A big rancher name of Harvey Niedenfuhr already claim to have the nomination in his pocket.

Some of us is disappointed by what's happened, but Bedelia Coyote is MAD. She is madder than all of us put together.

"It's really ironic," say Bedelia. "Here we been working to get Vic elected because we thought he had our interests at heart. Now he's gone and hooked up with Samantha and all of Chief

Tom's old cronies. After the election what we gonna have is a new chief, whose strings is still pulled by Samantha Yellowknees, except Vic is about three times smarter than Chief Tom, which make him three times as dangerous."

"And just as crooked."

"So what are we gonna do? The people are wild about Victor. Half the people who vote don't know or care who Samantha is."

"We're not gonna give up," shout Bedelia. "We're gonna have to do something I never thought I'd hear myself say. We're gonna have to side with Chief Tom."

We all groan. Then there is a silence go on for about four minutes. Nobody disagree with Bedelia, mainly the ten or so of us is just trying to figure out how we got in this position.

"I don't know," Frank finally say, "Chief Tom couldn't pour piss out of a boot, even if he had an instruction booklet in both official languages and Cree."

"Nobody ever said he was smart. But if we manage his campaign, we could keep him honest after he's elected. It's really Samantha we're fighting. But we have to contact every Indian on the reserve and explain why we've had to change our mind. I mean people believed us when we told them to vote for Victor."

We all travel off to Wetaskiwin and visit Chief Tom in his highrise apartment.

"Hey, Chief Tom," we say as we troop in, "we got some good news and some bad news for you."

"I only want to hear the good news," say the Chief. It plain to see he ain't shaved today and the apartment is a mess, dirty dishes and newspapers everywhere.

"I didn't know he shaved," say Connie Bigcharles.

"Well," say Frank, puff up his chest, smile like a TV anchorman.

"The good news is Constable Bobowski arrested Victor Ear for pissing in the snow."

Chief Tom smirk with one side of his face.

"That's hardly a serious crime," say the chief. "How did it happen?"

"He was outside the Blue Quills Hall after the dance last night, and he was spelling out VOTE VIC in the snow, when the Constable come along."

"Serves him right," say the chief.

"That brings us to the bad news," says Frank.

"What can be bad about Vic getting arrested?"

"Well, he wasn't alone."

"So?"

"The bad news is everybody recognize Samantha's handwriting in the snow."

We all laugh like maniacs. But Chief Tom, who look as pale and peaked as an Indian likely to get, actually let a tear trickle out of one of his eyes.

"I never suspected Chief Tom had feelings," whisper Connie.

"Even weasels have feelings," say Bedelia.

"Oh, young people," say Chief Tom, "I don't know what I'm going to do. I'm about to lose the election, and I've lost Samantha, and . . ." he snuffle up his face and actually go to crying.

"I'm sure you'll all be very happy to see me go. You won't have your old friend Chief Tom to kick around anymore."

"That's where you're wrong," say Frank. "We just formed the Chief Tom Crow-eye Admiration Society. We want you to keep on being chief. In fact I make up a slogan for you, The Chief of the Past is the Chief of the Future."

The Chief perk up visibly; he wipe his eyes and nose on his shirt-sleeve.

"But, young people, why do you all of a sudden want to help me? You've been opposed to me for years."

"We've been opposed to Samantha. We know you're not smart enough to dream up all the schemes you've been involved in."

"Thank you," say Chief Tom.

"So, since Samantha has deserted you for Victor Ear, we've decided you're the only person who can beat Samantha and Victor."

"Well, my friends," he say in a voice a little more like his own, "your gesture is supremely appreciated." He puff out his chest and go back to being his old self. "We will strike while the iron is hot. We will hunt down that elusive buffalo called Victory. When the going gets tough, the tough . . ."

"Where do we start?" ask Frank.

"Oh dear," say the chief. "I don't know. I've never run a campaign. If only Samantha were here. She'd know what to do," and his eyes get all watery again.

"You got to fight hard, Chief," we say. "How long you figure Samantha to stay with Victor Ear if he's the second place candidate?"

"We've got to think devious," say Bedelia. "We've got to think like Samantha. What would she do if she was on the Chief's side and he was behind in the election?"

"Desert him and go over to his opponent," say Frank.

"Maybe we could capitalize on his arrest," say the Chief.

"That was a joke," say Frank. "We was teasing you."

"Oh," say the Chief. "I'm afraid I never know what to take seriously."

"Well, you better take Victor Ear seriously. If you don't want to be on the list to work part-time cutting brush on railroad right-of-ways, you better dream up something," say Bedelia.

We talk for quite a while and decide that the answer is personal contact.

"We're gonna have to work harder than we've ever done before," say Bedelia. "We'll have to personally call on every eligible voter and make sure they know we've not only switched candidates, but that they understand why we've switched. We've got to beat Samantha and Victor. If they ever get into office we won't be able to blast them out with dynamite."

"I don't know," the Chief say, "the last thing Samantha told me was to keep a low profile."

"Is Vic keeping a low profile now that Samantha is managing him?"

"Well, no . . ."

"I'm still willing to be a candidate," say Frank. "I'll run as the Me First Party. My emblem will be a pig sitting on top of the world . . ."

"Listen!" Bedelia say to Chief Tom. "If we get you re-elected, you're gonna have to change your tune. No more fancy trips all over the world. You're going to have to work for the good of all us Indians."

"Young people, you have my word on it," say the chief.

"Yeah, that and a quarter will get you a telephone call."

"I won't make a move without your approval," Chief Tom go on. "Ms. Coyote, you just tell me what you want done. You and your friends will be my advisory board. And you'll be my personal assistant." He reach across the table and pat Bedelia's hand. "At a substantial salary, I may add."

Bedelia glare at him and pull her hand away.

"At a reasonable salary," say the chief.

Bedelia nod.

For the next three weeks we all work night and day. We contact every Indian eligible to vote, even track down ones who work away from the reserve. One afternoon me and Frank drive to a farm somewhere near Lacombe where a guy named Paul La Croix, who we hardly know, have a job as a hired hand. Turn out Paul drove a load of grain to the elevator, but the farmer invite us in to wait.

"You boys are Crees, are you?" he say to us.

"Not Crees anymore," say Frank. "We're the Fecawi Indians. Small independent tribe, short on numbers but long on courage."

"I didn't know the name," say the farmer, "but I remember how that chief took his little tribe back into the hills. Five or six years ago, wasn't it?"

"We're older than that," Frank continue. "About a hundred years ago we broke away from the Crees. Our leader was a warrior named Bulging Belly. Actually Bulging Belly was the first woman chief in Alberta. Though it come as a surprise to him that he was a woman. Bulging Belly's parents wanted a son, so they just kept her covered up and told her she was a boy. Originally she had another name, but it was by her bulging belly that she got found out.

"But her followers didn't mind. 'Go off to the hills and have a dream vision,' they said to Bulging Belly. 'Then you'll know what direction to lead us so we can find our promised land.'

"Bulging Belly went off to the hills to dream. She came back in eight days and said, 'I know what direction to lead you in so we'll have good hunting, warm weather, and much happiness.'

"'What will we call ourselves?' someone asked.

"'I'll tell you in good time,' said Bulging Belly. Then she gave the signal and led her little group of warriors on pinto ponies, off at a mad gallop across the prairie.

"They galloped for a few miles until Bulging Belly led them right over a high buffalo jump. They all landed in a cloud of dust, a heap of Indians, ponies, bones and buffalo chips.

"Bulging Belly pulled herself to her feet, looked around and gasped, 'Where the fuck are we?' And we been the Fecawi Indians ever since."

"You should be a comedian," the farmer say to Frank. "No," say Frank. "Comedians make up stories. I only speak the truth."

Bedelia write and rehearse some speeches for Chief Tom, so he don't sound totally ignorant at the next campaign meeting. Samantha and Victor want to have a public debate, but we shy away from that. Things still don't look good for us when election day come around. What we did do was tie a red bandanna around Chief Tom's head, get him to wear a buckskin jacket, though he insist on wearing the pants to his Conservative-blue suit and shiny shoes.

We spend all day hauling people down to the Blue Quills Hall so they can vote for Chief Tom. We have Louis Coyote's pickup truck, and Rufus Firstrider's 1957 Dodge with big green tail-fins and one back door missing.

Victor Ear and Samantha Yellowknees have rented for the day, a long white limousine, come from the Hertz stall at the Edmonton International Airport. They can haul about 20 bodies at a time, and people who have never voted in their life turn out just to get a ride in that fancy car, even some people we *know* is on our side. That is about all we have to feel good about.

We all hang around Blue Quills to see the counting is done honestly. It don't take long for us to start to feel better. Chief Tom build up about a ten-vote lead right away and hold that and even increase it as the evening wear on. The counting is all over, checked and rechecked, in about two hours and Chief Tom declared the winner by 27 votes.

After the announcement, the crowd, led by Frank and Connie, start chanting, "Crow-eye, Crow-eye, Crow-eye . . ."

Chief Tom shake Bedelia's hand, then mine, stand up and head to the platform. Lots of people cheer him. He smiles fit to bust his face.

Victor and Samantha been sitting at a table near the stage. Victor look kind of shocked, but he have an arm around Samantha's shoulder and whisper a lot into her ear. Samantha is busy writing on her clipboard, look as if her mind is on something else.

"My friends," Chief Tom begin. "I want to thank you all for re-electing me. You won't be sorry. My opponent fought a good fight and I congratulate him."

"We've got him, Silas," Bedelia say from across the table. "We're gonna be able to do things our way for a while."

"Most important of all," Chief Tom go on, "I want to thank my political advisor, who pulled victory from the jaws of defeat, and without whose brilliant planning I never could have triumphed. I owe her a great debt, for her keen political sense is solely responsible for my victory. I want her to come up here and share this auspicious moment with me."

Bedelia has been getting happier with each line Chief Tom speak. She is halfway out of her chair when the rest of what the Chief saying get through to her.

"Not only is she my political advisor, but she is the love of my life. Samantha, come up here, please."

Homer

One of my first memories is of *Uncle* Homer Hardy, though he sure wasn't my uncle, he being about as white as I'm Indian. Still I remember him being at our cabin, sitting sideways at the oilcloth covered kitchen table, his chewed-up-looking brown hat on his knee, him banging his coffee mug on the table to make a point, never once noticing the black coffee slopping over the top.

Homer was short, with fierce brown eyes buried in gray whiskers. A few strands of gray hair hung down the back of his neck, but he was mostly bald; his head was freckled, and what could be seen of his face was sun and windburned to the color of red willow.

"Homer's a prospector," my pa would say to us kids after Homer had left. I didn't understand about mining or gold, and it was a lot of years before I come to know what it was Homer did.

Usually he came by to try and get something from us, which, looking back, was not a smart idea, for there wasn't many people as poor as us.

"Paul," Homer would say to my dad, "I just need a grubstake. A few pounds of flour, some coffee, sugar if you can spare it. I'll shoot me rabbits for meat," and he'd nod toward the window, where, outside, his tall, buckskin horse munched grass, a .22-rifle in a leather scabbard just behind the saddle.

"I know where there's gold," Homer would say, and his eyes would blaze. "Back on the Nordegg River. Sittin' right there for the taking. You grubstake me, Paul, and we'll go ridin' into Wetaskiwin in a Cadillac automobile, lightin' our cigars with leftover ten-dollar bills," and Homer would smile, showing that his teeth was mostly missing, and his gums was the dark pink of ink erasers.

Pa would give Homer a few supplies. Ma would grumble, but she admit to me in recent years that she didn't mind too much. "It was like buying a ticket on the lottery nowadays. You know you ain't gonna win, but it give you somethin' to live for until next week or next month."

Homer would pack the groceries up in a canvas sack, and he'd smile and jig around just like a kid been given a new toy. He'd dig in the pockets of his overalls and come out with a few hard dimpled raspberry drops, or some triangular Vicks Cough Drops. They was used-looking and covered in lint and specks of tobacco dust, but boy, I remember how my mouth water while I'm seeing him search his pockets.

We wouldn't see Homer again for three or maybe six months. And when we did nothing would have changed. He wouldn't be rich, and if anybody asked, he'd just grin kind of sheepish and say, "That one didn't pan out like I figured. But I *know* where there's gold now. Right there for the takin' . . . ."

It was strange but no one I know ever felt cheated by Uncle

Homer. He would sweep in and out of the reserve, kind of like a one-man carnival—what he promised always being 100% more than he delivered.

One of the reasons everybody liked Homer Hardy was because he was a storyteller. In his saddlebag, in the front of a floppy black Bible, he carried a picture of his parents. In the middle-distance, in front of a sod house, a huge, barrel-chested, bald-headed man stood in knee-deep prairie grass, a slight, long-skirted woman with knitted eyebrows beside him.

"That's my papa, long before I was born. He walked to Utah with the Mormons. My mama was his fourth wife, a shirt-tail cousin of Brigham Young. Papa could play the fiddle and was the best jig-dancer in the Plains States. Why one time in Wyoming, Buffalo Bill heard about my papa and sent for him to come to his camp outside of Cheyenne somewheres. And papa went, played the fiddle and jig-danced like the devil himself. Buffalo Bill gave him a gold coin—a month's wages, my papa said it was.

"Another time papa was out herdin' sheep in Oregon, or maybe Utah, he was never too plentiful with details. He took his rifle out of the scabbard, dropped it accidental like, and it hit a rock and discharged. Shot him right here in the chest," and Homer'd grab the left side of his chest, while us kids, and my folks too, sat watching him, our mouths hanging open.

"Bullet went through his lung, and through to his back where he could feel the point of it pushing against his skin. Well, sir, he lay down in his little line-cabin and figured he was a goner. He took a pencil and wrote on his soft, brown cowboy hat, 'I shot myself accidental,' so's his wife, the one before my mama, wouldn't think he committed suicide.

"He lay there for over a week until a rancher happened by and found him. Nearest doctor was over forty miles away and they rode papa there in a buckboard. There weren't no roads, just went cross-country over the open range. He should of been dead six times but he wasn't. Doctor looked him over and said, 'This bullet's got to come out. You reckon you can stand it without anaesthetic?' "

Homer was like his daddy when it come to wives. He had at least four, maybe more.

"I never been ashamed of the fact that women find me attractive," he'd say, and smile, his eyes glinting like maybe some of the gold he spend his life lookin' for was in there.

Even Mad Etta like Homer Hardy. I was at her place one day maybe ten years ago when Homer Hardy turn up, driving an old, square-fendered truck, what used to be some color once, but was now just a sun-faded metallic.

"Etta," he say after she's fed him a meal and give him a cigarette. "Etta, if I just had enough money for a tire for my truck I could get that load of ore to Edmonton to the assay office, and none of us would ever have to work again."

Etta, she heard every hardluck story ever been told, and they roll off her broad back like a duck shed water. But next day Fred Crier down at Hobbema Texaco Garage put a new tire on Homer's truck, and I hear tell Etta, she rode down in the truck box, sitting on top of the ore, just so's she could pay for the tire. Also, Homer stayed overnight at Etta's cabin and some say she had a certain contented look about her, perched up there like a queen on that hill of chipped rock.

Homer's women was part of his stories. He never laugh at any of them, always at himself.

"First one should of knowed better," he say one time, "she

worked right in the assay office in Edmonton; she got to see the results from my samples. Her name was Bernice, a maiden lady, as we called them in the old days, and she was quite a bit older'n me. Come to think of it, all my wives have been a good bit older'n me," and he grin from behind his scratchy gray whiskers, what circle his face like a big vegetable brush.

People have been known to say that Homer married his wives for their money. Each one of them *had* money, at least when they married Homer Hardy. But Homer spend it on old trucks, and supplies, and mining equipment, pumps and generators, and lawyer fees for filing claims. Homer never deny that he gone through a lot of other people's money in his life.

"I could have settled in with any one of my wives and never worked again. I could have sat in Bernice's rooms there in the Kensington Apartments in Edmonton, but I'd of felt just like a gopher never come out of his hole, and besides, one of the reasons she married me was because I was dangerous. Women like to take risks, but they need somebody to push them along a little. Her eyes used to shine when I'd tell her about the gold we was going to wallow in. I'm real sorry I disappointed her. When her money was gone—she'd inherited a trunkful from her daddy who was one of the first managers of the Bank of Commerce in Edmonton—why she didn't have no choice but to throw me out. We stayed friends though. I was always welcome at her home, and she'd sometimes toss me a dollar or two to file a new claim. I hitchhiked all the way up from Montana when I heard she passed away. Was a day late for the funeral. But I went out there to Pleasantview Cemetery and stood by the flower-banked grave and said my goodbye. I think it was a good idea I was a day late. Her relatives would have been mortified. They never could figure what she saw in a bandy-legged prospector who only changes his underwear twice a year."

Homer he had stories about his other wives too, though he never did have a bad word to say about any of them.

Maybe five years ago he married for a fifth time, this time to an Indian lady, Martha Powderface. Martha was a widow lady, at least as old as Homer. Her family was wanting to put her in the Sundance Retirement Home in Wetaskiwin, but she married Homer and went with him to dig gold up on the Pembina River, and live in a tent on the riverbank.

"You know, Silas," Homer said to me the next year, "it's too bad Martha doesn't have money. Oh, now I don't mean that as a criticism. I just mean that if, fifty years ago, I'd had a woman *with money* who'd go out to the camp with me, I'd a been successful. I'd a made the earth give up the gold it keeps hiding from me. Martha's a good woman, Silas."

Uncle Homer was a musician of sorts himself; he could play the spoons. Spoon players, like prospectors, are few and far between these days. In fact, when I think about it, I don't know a single person able to take two teaspoons, and by holding them in one hand in some mysterious way, clack the undersides together to make music. A good spoon player can sound pretty close to a banjo, and a harmonica and spoon player can sound like a whole Western band.

Homer would no sooner be in the door of our cabin than we'd be beggin' him to play and sing for us. And I can remember seeing my sister run for the spoon drawer, where all the knives and forks and other cutlery was kept, when we heard the wheels of Homer's wagon creaking up the hill from Hobbema.

"Sing about the fly," we'd yell, and Homer Hardy would smile from under his chewed up hat, clack the spoons and sing:

The early fly's the one to swat,
He comes before the weather's hot,
And sits around and files his legs,
And lays about 10,000 eggs.

And every egg will hatch a fly,
To drive us crazy by and by,
Yet every fly that skips our swatters,
Will have 10,000,000 sons and daughters,
And countless first and second cousins,
And aunts and uncles scores and dozens.

That song went on for about 20 minutes, or at least it seemed like it to us kids—there was verses and verses, and we'd laugh and giggle, and Illianna would sit on Homer's knee, and pretend she was looking for insects in his beard, and finding them. And my brother Thomas, who was the baby then, lay on the floor in blue rompers, grinning from his toothless little mouth.

Other songs were about people his father grew up with; the names and places didn't mean anything to us, but the tune was always snappy:

When I was working on the ditch,
Near Shell, for Isaac Jones,
I got acquainted with a boy,
Who runs the gramophone,
He was a charming little lad,
And his mama called him Sweet,
But I had no idea that,
His Waterloo he'd meet,
His Waterloo he'd meet.

There was about 50 verses to that song too. And sometimes we'd all join in, even my pa, who was never very sociable, and like me had a voice flat as a prairie.

One time I was telling Old Miss Waits, my teacher from the Reserve School, about Homer, and what a wonderful storyteller he was.

"He claims he never been to school," I said. "Taught himself to read by having a friend print the alphabet, then matching up letters with those he found in the Bible."

"I suppose that's *possible*," said Miss Waits. "You know, Silas, one negative aspect of education is that it destroys the natural storyteller in us, for education makes us aware of our own insignificance. Our own life story, unless it is particularly bizarre or magical, becomes uninteresting beside what we have learned. The uneducated person, however, is still at the center of his limited universe, and not only considers his life experience worth repeating, but will do so without invitation."

At the time I just stared at Miss Waits and tried to remember how she strung together them big words. But now that I've had a few years to think about it, I agree with her. When I was a kid nobody on the reserve had TV and only a few had radios. We make our own jokes. I remember the time Collins One-wound was sitting on his corral fence smoking a cigarette, just gazing at the cattle and mud, when one of his kids, might have been David, or maybe even my girl, Sadie, though I doubt it was Sadie 'cause she always been real shy, sneaked up behind Collins walking soft as if they wearing moss moccasins, and go "Boo!" real loud.

Collins, whose mind I guess be a thousand miles away, fall forward like he been shot, and when he stand up he is covered in corral muck from head to foot. That story go around the reserve for days, and everybody who hear it laugh and laugh, slap their hands on their thighs, have to wipe tears out of their eyes. Even today, must be 15 years later, Collins One-wound is still called "Muddy" by some people.

Since television and movies and cars with stereo players come along, falling in the mud in a corral ain't near as funny as it used to be.

Homer Hardy thinks his life has been interesting and he tell about it every chance he get, and because *he* thinks it is interesting, it *is*.

One time Homer he took me with him on a mining trip. He had a piece of tattered paper in his saddlebag he claim to show the location of the Lost Lemon Mine, a story everybody in the West know about.

"Back almost a hundred years ago two miners named Lemon and Blackjack went into the mountains down near the Montana border, and they struck gold," is the way Homer Hardy told the story. "The biggest strike you could imagine," and Homer would ball up his fists to show how big the nuggets was that Lemon and Blackjack found.

"At their camp Lemon went crazy and he killed his partner, and he rode away with just a few nuggets. He was raving when he reached civilization, though his pockets was full of gold to back up his story. But try as he might, he never could lead folks back to the spot where him and Blackjack found the gold. Men is still lookin' for that lode." Homer paused as dramatically as if he was an actor on stage. "But I know the *real* story," he go on. "Two young Indians was hiding in the bush and watched the murder. They rode off and told their chief what they'd seen. One was named Crow Mountain, and the other took the name Kills Him Alone, because of what he'd seen, and nobody ever spoke his former name again. The old chief, Red Ears, was a wise man; he looked into the future and seen thousands of us palefaces ruining his hunting and tearing down his mountains piece by piece, so he swore the two braves to silence for the rest of their days. Then he had them ride out and move the campsite, Blackjack's body, and generally change the terrain so no one would ever be able to find that gold mine.

"But I'm gonna find it. And you're gonna help me, Silas. I got this here map from Red Ears' grandson; had to trade my truck and a case of whiskey for it, but it's the real thing. What are you gonna do with your million dollars, Silas?"

There is something about the word *gold* that makes the blood run faster, and makes your eyes kind of glaze over with hope. I don't know when I ever been so excited as in the days we making the trip from Hobbema to the Montana mountains. Where we going was off in the bush beyond a coal mining town called Blairmore. I remember looking at the mountain and feeling all tingly, seeing the trees angling up the ridge in single file, hitched together by shadows like a packtrain.

But once we got there it was sure different—it rained and the sun, when it did shine, was hot; the air was alive with mosquitoes and black flies, and it ain't no fun to eat half-raw fish over a sickly fire. That land was a lot tougher than we was. After two weeks we limped home—and ever since I been content to buy a lottery ticket when I get the urge to be wealthy. But it didn't faze Homer one bit, he just rest up until his rheumatism was better and his insect bites healed and off he go again.

Two years ago about now Homer had his accident. Him and Martha Powderface was prospecting a little river somewhere in the Rocky Mountain House country, when Homer slip as he scrambling over river rocks and break his leg, not just in one, but in two places.

"I'd a been a goner if it wasn't for Martha," he tell us afterward. "She rigged up a travois out of saplings and tent canvas, and she drug me over fifteen miles of rough country to where we'd parked the truck. And you know what? Martha had never drove in her life. But she's a quick learner," and he smiled across the little studio apartment in the Sundance Retirement Home, where they was living now, to where Martha was cooking oatmeal on the tiny white stove.

"Lucky that truck could be driven in Cree," Homer go on, and he laugh, showing where his teeth used to be, and Martha smile too, from under the flowered babushka she's taken to wearing over her white hair lately.

Homer is pretty well tied to his chair in front of the 12" TV. Between his broke leg and his rheumatism he need two crutches just to move the five steps to the bathroom. But his troubles don't stop him from dreaming.

"The streets of Edmonton are paved with gold. That ain't no lie. They gravelled them with rock right out of the North Saskatchewan River, and you could see the glint of gold in the first pavement of Jasper Avenue, and Whyte Avenue. One time I took my jackknife and dug a nugget the size of the moon on my thumbnail out of Whyte Avenue right at the corner of 104th Street."

One of Martha's sons, Eagle Powderface, listen to enough of Homer's stories that he get fired up to try his hand at prospecting.

But his enthusiasm run dry, just like mine, when he actually have to live in the rain, wind, and cold of the mountains for weeks at a stretch. Besides that, he never find any gold.

I guess prospecting is a little like storytelling, it ain't as much fun since life got easier and information more plentiful.

About two weeks ago I heard Uncle Homer was in the hospital. But before I could even get up to see him he was back at Sundance Retirement.

"Doctors just opened him up, took a look, and sewed him closed again," says Mad Etta. "I went over and took a gander at him, but there ain't no cure for old age."

The next night, though there is a wicked blizzard blowing, me and Sadie stop by Homer and Martha's place. Mad Etta travel with us, wrapped in a buffalo coat and covered in a tarp, she covered in about an inch of snow by the time we get from the reserve to Wetaskiwin. Homer has sure failed bad since I seen him last. He is propped up on pillows in the convertible sofa-bed, look shorter than I ever remember, his toes poking the bedclothes only halfway down the sheet, his whiskers ermine-white now, and his scalp pale, freckles like wheat grains scattered on his skull.

But he's still tellin' stories. Even has one I haven't heard.

"When I was just a boy in Wyoming, only twelve about, soon as the trees started budding, papa sent me and my brother up into the hills with our ponies, a packhorse drooping with grub, and about five hundred head of stock. Ben, he was a year older'n me; we rode herd on them cattle until round-up time. Never saw another soul all summer. There was a small buckaroo cabin, not much more than a log shelter, but someplace for us to put our bedrolls down out of the rain.

"The spring I was sixteen, when we came to that cabin, it was one terrible scene. Sometime in the winter, a wild mustang had pushed the door open in order to take shelter. Wind probably blew the door closed behind him. He'd died maybe a month before. Ain't no words to describe the smell. And you ever tried to get a dead, falling-apart horse out of a tiny cabin door? 'He must of had to kneel down to get in,' is what my brother said.

"Well, we lassoed his legs and tried to pull him out piece by piece, but we wasn't too successful, and as luck would have it, it rained a lot and we sure needed some shelter. Worst job of my life gettin' that carcass out of there. And the smell of death stayed with that cabin all summer. We finally covered the floor with cow chips," and when he see Sadie wrinkle up her nose at that idea, he go on, "You never figured cow chips would smell sweet, would you? Well they did. And they soaked up the odor of death." He pause for a few seconds. "I reckon Martha may have to do the same with this place in a week or two," and he kind of wink across the crowded room at Martha Powderface.

Homer rest for a while, but the wind that was blowing snow hard against the small window by his head wake him again. He must have been dreaming about someplace else, because he have a surprised look on his tired face.

"It's out there, Silas," he say. "Eagle, it's out there right now, even in the winter, in the snow. Little flecks of sunshine trapped in rock, lighting up the night. With gold in your poke you'll never be cold. All you need to get is a blowtorch. It's there. And I know right where it is."

Homer lay his head back on the pillow. Martha Powderface pull the cover up under his chin.

A Hundred Dollars' Worth of Roses

My mother, before she married Paul Ermineskin, was Suzie Buffalo. Her family all moved away from the reserve long before I was born. My grandparents have been dead a long time too. I guess Ma mentioned once or twice that we got an Uncle Wilf, but it don't sink in very deep.

I'm sitting in the sun in front of our cabin when this strange dude come hoofin' it up the hill. He's maybe 50, healthy-looking and muscular; he's packing an expensive saddle, and a black suitcase covered in a layer of red and yellow stickers. That suitcase got the names of more cities on it than most maps.

"Which is Suzie Ermineskin's place?" he ask me, squint one eye against the sunshine.

"You found it. But she's off to Wetaskiwin for the day. I'm her son, Silas."

"Silas, eh? You named after the guy in the Bible who spent a lot of time in jail?"

"No. My mom had a brother, died as a baby. They thought they'd give his name another chance."

"I knew him," the stranger say. "Only lived for ten days. Me and Max Buffalo built the coffin. Big Etta lived for the whole ten days at our cabin; tried every trick she knew to save that baby. Say, is Etta still around?"

"Sure is," I say, and point up the hill where Etta's cabin sit back in the poplars.

"I'm sort of your uncle," he say, set down the saddle and stick out a thick-fingered hand for me to shake. "My folks died when I was a baby; Max Buffalo and his wife, your grandparents, raised me as one of their own. Wilf Cuthand is how your mom would know me, though I've never been a guy to keep with one name for long," and he smile a big, open smile, show a lot of happy lines around his eyes and mouth.

Before Ma gets home, Wilf Cuthand has made a friend out of me. He is really interested to hear I write books, and when I go and get one he look it over real careful.

"By god," he say, "you know this is one thing I ain't done that I should have. I'm going to have to write a book about my life."

I can see that he means what he says. Then he tell me a story about something that happened to him at the Cheyenne Rodeo 20 years or so ago. A gambler want him to throw the calf-roping event, an event Wilf is the heavy favorite to win; that gambler offer more cash than first prize money for Wilf to lose, 'cause he got a bet on somebody else to win.

"I took his cash, then I went out and won the event anyway," Wilf says. "That guy was so mad I thought he was gonna kill me right behind the chutes. 'Let's go in the tack room and talk,' I said to him. He agree, grinning kind of sly 'cause he's dying to get me alone. Soon as we're inside that storeroom he pull a blue gun from inside his coat. 'I'm gonna shoot your knees off, cowboy,' he says to me. 'You're gonna be sorry for the rest of your life that you double-crossed me.'

"Just as he's aiming the gun at me about fifteen cowboys stand up from behind the packing boxes. 'They're all unarmed,' I told him. 'But the way we figure it, you got at most six bullets in your gun. Killing cowboys is like shooting tumbleweeds—so there'll be about a dozen of us left when you're out of bullets. You must have seen a car stripped down slow and smooth by experts. That's how we're gonna take you apart unless you start running in the direction of Phoenix, and promise never to attend another rodeo in your life.'

"We meant what we said about him travelin' on foot. We'd boxed his car in. You know nobody ever claimed it. At least not while the rodeo was in Cheyenne. And no one ever heard of that gambler again."

Wilf laugh a deep, hearty laugh as he finish up the story.

I'm kind of surprised that, when Ma gets home, she ain't near as excited to see Wilf as I would have expected.

"Oh, it's you," is what she said after she come in the cabin door and seen Wilf sitting across the kitchen table from me, a mug of coffee in his hand.

"I know it's only been thirty years, but I thought you might at least be surprised," said Wilf. "Boy, talk about your stoic Indian."

Ma get a smile around the edges of her face.

"I always knew you'd turn up. Why should I be surprised?" she say. But when Wilf Cuthand stand up from the table, tip his beat-up kitchen chair over backward and hug Ma to him, picking her right off her feet and swinging her around, she don't put up a struggle; she even laugh. Something I realize Ma ain't done a lot in her life. But all that evening Ma keep a wary eye on Wilf like she afraid he going to steal something from us.

"I was down in Newfoundland a couple of years ago," he say at the supper table. "I was supposed to be on that *Ocean Ranger*, you know, the oil rig that sunk. I lost a lot of good friends. I had some time off and I went to the mainland, met this girl in Halifax. Somehow I was a day late reporting back for work. Hey, I phoned up this flower shop and I sent that girl a hundred dollars' worth of roses."

"Did you marry her?" ask Delores, my littlest sister.

"No. I didn't even plan to see her again. I just wanted her to know I appreciated her saving my life."

"Hmmmmmfff," say Ma, get up from the table, take her plate to the kitchen counter.

I bet there's hardly a place Wilf Cuthand ain't been at one time or another.

"I'm curious," he says, cutting into a slice of saskatoon pie. "There ain't nothin' worse than a person who ain't curious. You know what a cat's like when you place him in a strange house; he explores everything real careful. I been that way with the world. I've been like a cat exploring all the strange rooms of the world."

And he tell us a story about how he was a paratrooper during the Korean War, and how he float down behind enemy lines on a cold, clear winter night.

"I'm gonna see the world," say Delores. "I'm gonna do Indian dances all over the world."

"She's real good," I say. "Dances in a group called the Duck Lake Massacre."

"You've got the right idea," says Wilf. "You dance for me one of these days. I might be able to show you a trick or two. I was a pretty fair thunder-dancer when I was young. And Delores, you plan now to have your own dancing troupe when you're grown up: the Delores Ermineskin Dancers. You can do it if you set your mind to it."

By the time I've known him for a few days I've decided Wilf really has had enough experiences to write a book. He is as full of stories as I am, except his are truer than mine. He claim to have fought oil-well fires with Red Adair, the most famous oil-well fire-fighter in the world. He tell of once walking right into the center of a fire, all dressed up in an asbestos suit. Nobody who hadn't been there could describe it so believably. He knows too, how to pilot a helicopter. He been to Africa and drove a jeep alongside a herd of 10,000 wildebeests and zebras.

"Weren't you scared?" Connie Bigcharles ask him one after-noon at the pool hall. "How did you know where to start?" Con-nie is Frank's girlfriend and she ain't one to admit being afraid.

"You have to keep asking yourself questions," Wilf say. "Is it better to stay where I am or better to go to strange places?"

"You must have always chose the strange place," says Connie.

"Connie, what do you want to do more than anything else in the world?"

"I want to be an actress and see myself on the TV. I want to wear pretty clothes like actresses do."

"Why can't you do that?"

"I don't know how."

"Do you know where there's a TV station?"

"Yes. There are two or three in Edmonton. More in Calgary."

"Why don't you go to one of them and ask for a job?"

"Oh, I'd be too shy. They wouldn't have any work for me. I'm an Indian. I'd be too scared."

"Scared! Let's have a little ceremony. Everybody speak the word *scared* into their hand, then we toss it on the floor and stomp on it." Wilf do just that. Delores follow him quick, and in a minute so do Connie and Frank, Rufus and Winnie Bear, even me. "How do you think I got a job with Red Adair?" Wilf go on. "How do you think I got into the movies and TV? I walked right up, scared as I was, pretended I knew what I was doing, and *asked* for work."

"You did?"

"Sure. When I felt my knees shaking I just thought, Hey, I got rid of that word scared. It don't exist no more. 'What experience have you had?' Mr. Adair said to me. 'I was a firefighter for seven years in Bismarck, North Dakota,' I said. 'It's a tradition among the Sioux, just as the Mohawks are steelworkers, the Sioux are firefighters.' Red Adair squinted at me and half smiled. I don't know whether he believed me or admired my ability as a liar. 'You got yourself a job,' he said. 'Thank you, Mr. Adair,' I said. 'My name's Joe Dynamite.'"

The conversation continued back at our cabin at suppertime.

"That was all there was to it? You just walked up and asked for every job you ever got?" said Connie.

"Well, I got turned down ten times for every job I landed. But you got to have stamina too, and thick skin. Every time somebody said something mean to me I just pretended to grow another layer of skin so next time it wouldn't hurt so much. By now I got almost fifty layers of skin. Nothin' affects me anymore. Hell, there ain't anything mysterious about what I've got to say. You can do whatever you set your mind on doing," and he shift Delores from one knee to another where he been bouncing her like she riding a bucking horse.

"You believe I could be an actress like the girls I see on TV?" says Connie.

"If you want it bad enough. Most people are all talk and wishes. Listen, there's an old Navajo saying, 'If you want something and you don't know how to get it, then you don't want it bad enough.' We've all got to dream, and we got to have heroes or we ain't anything at all. Dreaming of heroes is what life is all about. Anyone can be like their heroes if they really set their mind to it."

"J.R. Ewing is my hero," says Frank. "Could I be like him? Rich and mean with beautiful women standing in line to shine my Mercedes."

"No, you couldn't," says Wilf.

"But you said . . . ."

"You could be rich if you set your mind to it. Seems to me you already got more women than your fair share. But you couldn't be mean. You've got a soft center, just like my girl Delores here," and he tickle her ribs to make her giggle. "Almost everybody here got a soft center—Silas, Winnie Bear, Rufus—seem like Suzie is the only one got a flint arrowhead where her heart ought to be." We all stare over at Ma, who been doing dishes in the blue enamel dishpan. Ma bang a couple of plates together, real hard, and keep on with her work.

"Tell us another story," Delores say to Wilf at supper a couple of days later. "I like your stories better than Silas'," she go on with that painful honesty little kids have.

"Let me tell you a little bit about my movie days," Wilf say. "By the way, I agree with Delores," and he wink at me. "Silas, you're okay as a storyteller, but you better hope I never decide to go into competition with you. You guys must have seen me in the movies or on TV, without even knowing me. Back in the fifties, when there were lots of westerns on TV, why I was in about two shows a week. Every time they wanted an Indian I'd be there. I'd wrap a blanket around myself and be eighty years old, or I'd whip off my jeans and shirt and run across the set in only a loincloth. I'd wear braids, or long hair with a headband and lots of eagle feathers. My name would appear way at the bottom of the credits:

Sixth Indian: Thomas Many Guns

"I made a good living doing that. I liked TV 'cause you only had to do things once, or twice at the most. Some of the shows we did were live. In movies you had to do a scene maybe forty times, until it didn't feel natural anymore. At the end of one movie we were making, I was supposed to walk off into the sunset with people waving goodbye to me. I walked down a path and turned left about twenty-five times, but the director kept having me repeat the scene. 'I want you to turn right next time,' he told me. I could see having to do twenty-five takes turning right. I walked down the path and turned left again. 'You were supposed to turn the other way,' the director hollered. 'I'm an Indian and it's Sunday,' I called back. 'Indians can't turn right on Sunday.' The director thought that over for a minute, then said, 'Okay, let's print it.'"

We all laugh and pound our thighs at that story.

"Seems like Suzie's the only one here don't like me," Wilf says.

Ma been sitting back in the darkness by the cookstove. Seem to me she got her babushka tied tighter around her head these days.

"If you're such a big wheel," she say harshly, "how come you got nothin' to show for it? For fifty-some years all you got to show is the clothes on your back and a bagful of stories sounds more like Silas' lies than truth to me."

Wilf stay silent for a minute. It the first time I seen him taken aback by anything since he got here.

"Suzie, you know what I've got to show for fifty-five years? I'm happy. I don't know how many people in the world can say that. My guess is not very many. You know how tough we had things when we were kids—well I didn't let that bother me. I just said to myself, I'm not going to wait around to see what life will bring me; I'm gonna go out and meet life. I done it. And I'm not sorry. Most people my age have lived one year fifty-five times. I've lived fifty-five separate years, and I'm gonna live every one that's left to me the same way. And I'm trying to teach your kids and their friends to follow my example. I don't apologize for it."

"Hmmmfff," go Ma, from her dark corner, but I'm not sure if the sound is scornful or if she's sniffing back tears.

A few days later, Wilf, who living in with Dolphus Fryingpan, because Dolphus have an extra bed in his cabin, show us an example of not taking no for an answer.

"You and me are goin' to the dance Saturday night at Blue Quills Hall," he tell Ma.

"I'm not," says Ma.

"I'm taking you," Wilf say. "Whether you get dressed up or not is up to you. I'll be by to get you at eight o'clock. You know, Silas," he say to me, "when your mom was young she was the best polka dancer in a hundred miles. An old man name of Conrad Raven used to fiddle and we used to dance until we pounded dust out of the floorboards of the community hall."

I've never thought of Ma as ever being young, though it reasonable that she was. She's never even had a boyfriend in all the years since Pa left us. I guess children don't like to think of their parents as being real people.

I am surprised as anything at the way Ma look that night. She chucked her head scarf, and her hair, that I only ever seen untied when she washed it, is combed out and fanned over the shoulders of a white blouse she borrow from Sadie.

That is something else that surprise me: Ma being able to wear Sadie's clothes. I've always thought of Ma as big, huge even. I know she only stand to my shoulder, but parents always seem big to kids.

Ma's blue-black hair got a few silver threads in it. I mean, I just never knew she was pretty. She wear a bright green skirt and green shoes she got from Connie Bigcharles. Ma usually wear a shapeless, colorless dress and brown stockings.

Wilf wear a pearl-colored western shirt and a silver buckle the size of a small book that engraved "Grand Forks Rodeo, All Round Cowboy, 1960." He polished that buckle until it shine like chrome on a new car.

"You're twice as pretty as the woman I took to the Academy Awards Dinner back in '62. I was in a picture that was nominated that year. I paid a guy a thousand bucks for his tickets, figured it was something everybody should do once in their life."

It is the first time I ever seen Ma do more than one dance with anybody. She never get to sit down from one end of the evening to the other. When there is a Virginia Reel, me and Sadie get in the same group and I dance with Ma for the first time in my life, even if it is just joining elbows and swinging in a circle.

Wilf and Ma stomped up a storm all that night at Blue Quills, and Ma is just as good a dancer as he said. Ma was really shy at first and Wilf about had to carry her onto the floor for the first waltz of the evening.

It is also the first night since I can remember that Ma gets in later than me. Day is pushing pink light in the windows when Ma come in. I hear Wilf say something about breakfast, but Ma shush him and send him on his way. I know Dolphus Fryingpan is off on the rodeo circuit, so it ain't too hard to figure where Ma and Wilf been for the past four hours or so.

"It's about time Suzie got herself a man," Mad Etta said that evening at Blue Quills, from where she sat high up on her tree-trunk chair, alongside the Coke machine.

And over the next couple of weeks it does look like Suzie Ermineskin has got herself a man. Her and Wilf spend almost every night together, though she never bring him to her bed. It seem funny, but I've brought Sadie home for years and years, but Ma don't feel right to bring her boyfriend home. They even go to Edmonton for a weekend where they stay at the Chateau Lacombe Hotel, go to the movies and to fancy restaurants for steak and Chinese food.

"It's like old times," say Wilf at Hobbema Pool Hall one afternoon. "Except in the old days, when your Ma and me was young, we didn't have two pennies to rub together. Though we were raised in the same house Suzie and me weren't related. Way back in those days I liked her a whole lot. I wanted her to go with me when I hit the road. I asked her to go with me." I guess Wilf can see my eyes get wide. "She was the prettiest and smartest girl on the reserve. I was afraid for both of us if we stayed, her more than me . . ." and his voice trail off.

The pool hall is completely silent. We is all standing like we was in a photograph, waiting for him to go on.

"She turned me down. It was simple as that. I even offered to get married if she'd come with me. Only time in my life I ever proposed to a woman. She was afraid of what was out there. I was afraid too, but the difference was I couldn't wait to find out what it was I was afraid of."

Wilf has by now got us all dreaming. Rufus admit he always wanted to be a bartender.

"Well, you can be," say Wilf. "A mixologist is what it's called. All it takes is a little nerve. You look up *Bartending Schools* in the Yellow Pages, call and find out how much it costs. Save your money. Enroll. Nothing's stopping you but yourself. After you graduate you go to hotels and big restaurants and sell yourself. Don't go whispering 'I'm an Indian,' or trying to pretend you're not. Say 'I'm the first Indian bartender in Alberta. Let me make you a drink called a Chicken Dancer . . .'"

"But I wouldn't . . .," say Rufus.

"You'd make it up. Play it by ear. Take a chance."

Wilf do the same thing to each of us. I'm thinking of trying to get an agent to really sell my books to big publishers and to the movies and TV. And Frank admit he want to own an auto-wrecking and second-hand business. Wilf got good answers to all our questions and objections.

"But we're Indians," somebody say.

This is the only time since he been here Wilf lose his patience.

"You can be a success and still be an Indian," he say real sharp. "Don't any of you ever use being an Indian as an excuse for failure. People are people wherever you go. Indian, Black, White, Yellow, doesn't make a damn bit of difference what color you are outside. It's what you've got inside that counts. The failures all excuse themselves by saying 'I'm just a poor Indian, what do you expect,' a whiner's a whiner, a loser's a loser, white or Indian," and he look around fierce at us, his eyes flashing.

"What do you figure's gonna happen with Ma and Wilf?" I ask Mad Etta.

Etta look at me for a long time. I feel like her old eyes are drilling holes in my chest.

"You know," she says.

"I do?"

"If I thought you were dumb I wouldn't of made you my assistant."

"What do I know?"

Etta smile deep in her face. "That Wilf is like the first soft weather of March; weather that turn the snowbanks soft as putty, put the smell of life in the air, set us to dreaming of summer."

"But what you're describing is called a false spring."

"Good," says Etta. "I told you you knew."

A few nights later Ma come home about midnight. Everyone else is in bed; the rooms in our cabin been made by hanging blankets on clothesline cord. Sadie is snuggled down deep in the quilts beside me. Ma make herself coffee and sit at the table a long time. I doze off, but wake as the cabin door close. I recognize Wilf's boots on the kitchen floor. Wilf has been carrying his suitcase. I can hear the metal edges clack as he sit it down on the linoleum.

"What do you want now?" says Ma. Her voice is tired.

"I came to say goodbye. And I come to apologize if I made you unhappy. I know you don't like what I been selling to the young people. Are you sorry I came back, Suzie?"

"No. I guess not," Ma say after a long pause.

"Are you afraid of me?"

After an even longer pause Ma says, "No. I'm afraid of me."

"I know. If I don't leave now I might never leave. I'm too old to put down roots. Yours are too deep in the ground to be pulled up . . . ."

I've never really thought of what Ma has missed out on. She's been like a windbreak for us kids. She's done whatever she could to help us, mainly she just kept us together, when over half the families on the reserve fell apart. She never let white social workers get their hooks into our family.

"What if . . . what if I was to come back in a few years, when Delores is on her own and you're as free as you were thirty-five years ago? Think you might travel a little with me?"

"I don't know," say Ma.

"It'll be something for both of us to dream about. Something to keep us going. Even if it don't work out it's better to wake up than not to dream at all. All the time I been here I been telling the young folks to find someone to look up to. Dreaming of heroes ain't such a bad occupation.

"Suzie, you don't think I know what you've done here. But I do. You chose a harder life than me, and you stuck it out in a way I might not have been able to. You've lived your life for your kids. I've lived my life mostly for me. The wisest thing you ever did was turn me down all those years ago. I think maybe you saved my life."

"You gonna send me a hundred dollars' worth of roses?" say Ma, and her voice is younger than I think I ever heard it. It is a girl's husky voice, no older than Connie's or Sadie's.

"Would you like that?"

"I don't know." But Ma's voice catches as she says it. There is a long silence and it would be my guess that they are holding onto each other.

"Keep lookin' out the window there, Suzie. Keep lookin' down the hill to the highway. One day a panel truck from Boxmiller Flower Shop in Wetaskiwin will come driving slow up the hill.

Painted on the side of that panel truck is a picture of a guy with a funny helmet on his head and wings on his heels. The driver will have a hundred dollars' worth of roses for you."

"No," says Ma, and I can tell she is crying. "There's other things we need. Delores . . . ."

"They'll be for Suzie Ermineskin and nobody else. You've spent all your life giving. There won't be any card. You just think of this old man with wings on his feet . . . ."

I hear Wilf walk across the floor, stop and pick up his suitcase and saddle, then head out the door.

Ma pull up a chair and sit at the kitchen table. She blow out the lamp. I can see tines of moonlight strung across the floor. I cuddle down in my bed. It gonna be nice, seeing Ma staring down the road, dreaming.

The
Medicine Man's
Daughter

M y friend Frank Fencepost insists that the most feared words in either English or Cree are not *"You're under arrest,"* or, *"Guilty as charged,"* but, *"I'm pregnant."* Frank also claim that since he started making it with girls, which he says was when he was ten, that the most popular names on the reserve is Frank for boys and Frankie for girls. Frank is the kind of guy who, when both of Elias Stonechild's twin daughters come around claiming they is pregnant and that Frank is the father, say, "Hey, I was only joking. You guys took something seriously that was poked at you in fun."

Frank figure it is his duty to get as many girls pregnant as possible.

"If my kids are all as smart as me, Fenceposts will rule the world in a couple of generations," he say, and laugh hearty.

It is a good thing that Frank's more-or-less steady girlfriend, Connie Bigcharles, was already on the birth control pills when they met.

"If you want babies, *you* have them," is what Connie says. "I'll consider getting pregnant, right after you bought us a four-bedroom house and a Cadillac."

Frank grumble and mumble and talk about wasting his valuable assets, and that having sex with a girl who ain't liable to get pregnant is like building a dog-house when you ain't got a dog.

"Anytime you want to change dog-houses, you just let me know," says Connie. "You ain't the only fish swimmin' under the bridge."

Connie is the only person who can treat Frank like that and get away with it. If she cried or got sulky when Frank fools around with someone else, he'd dump her in a minute. But Connie is just as happy go lucky as Frank. She goes off with somebody she likes once in a while too. And don't Frank get mad. But it don't do him no good.

"What would you rather I do," Connie ask him, "go off and have a good time when I'm mad at you, or sit home waiting with a shotgun and blow your peter all the way to Saskatchewan the next time you show up?"

Frank cross his legs, grin, and say, "Have a good time."

With me and Sadie things are different. It was me who got Sadie to go on the birth-control pills. I seen a poster at the Tech School in Wetaskiwin, tell about the Free Clinic that held there once a week. I'd just started at Tech School, I was 16 and Sadie 14, and the last thing we needed in our life was babies. The school on the reserve is run by the Catholic Church, and they do their best to keep everyone ignorant about sex. Sadie is so shy I had to practically drag her to that clinic, go inside and sit with her, answer most of the questions the nurse ask, and do everything but go into the examining room with her.

That was almost five years ago, and everything's run smooth since then. The clinic sell birth control pills at cost—sometimes me and Sadie had to collect pop bottles and sell them to make the buy, but we always managed.

That is why it was such a shock to me, when, one night in the coldest part of March, right after we come out of the Alice Hotel from having a few beers, Sadie slide over beside me on the seat of Louis Coyote's pickup truck and, the cold air coming out her mouth like smoke, say, "I been to the clinic twice this week and the doctor says I'm pregnant."

I didn't say anything for quite a while.

"Do you think we'll get married?" Sadie say, as I easing the truck out onto the highway.

"I'm trying to figure how it could have happened," I say. "Did they give us some bad pills, or did you forget to take them proper?"

"I didn't forget," Sadie say in a small voice.

"Then they must have sold us bad stock. I think they sell samples, stuff they're given, some of it's probably pretty old."

"I guess," said Sadie.

"Sure we'll get married," I said. There was a bitter wind, and snow was blowing in sheets across the highway, cutting my visibility to almost nothing.

"I'm glad," said Sadie, and she laid her head against my shoulder.

"It's about time you two joined the population explosion," Frank say when I tell him. I don't quite understand why, but it has taken me three days to get around to telling him. "Hey, you can read to it right through Sadie's belly, and it'll be born writing books like its old man. Don't laugh, you ever seen how many books there are in the children's section of the library? There must be a lot of kids who write."

I give a polite laugh.

"You sure don't look very happy," Frank go right on. "Don't worry about the wedding. Fencepost, your best man, will take care of all the details. Nothing is too good for my best friend. You'll name the baby Frank Fencepost Ermineskin, of course. Venison. We'll have venison steaks at the reception. Your sister Delores and her dancing troupe can perform. I'll look after the bar. At cost. Well, almost at cost. And as a grand finale, Robert Coyote and Gaston Sixkiller will blow up a bridge on Highway 2A. Memorable, huh?"

"Yeah, memorable," I say.

"Hey, if you don't want to get married I can help too. Fencepost is a master of disguise. I can change your appearance so you won't even know you, let alone anybody else. You'll be able to live right here on the reserve. First thing you have to do is take that row of pens out of your shirt pocket . . . ."

"Frank, this is serious," I say.

"What's the matter? You figure it's not yours? I read where they can run tests. I'll take a lie-detector test; it wasn't me. I wouldn't do that to you. I got morals. Besides Sadie hates my guts."

"I just don't understand how it could have happened."

"I read about that too, there's these here eggs and sperms . . ."

"I know you're trying to cheer me up, but just can it, alright? If I thought it was really an accident we'd be married by now," I said.

"You better hash this out with Sadie. Maybe talk to a doctor."

"I already been to that clinic in Wetaskiwin. 'It can happen,' the nurse at the clinic told me. But she look at me out of the corner of her eye when she say that. Either it can't happen, or she just thinks Sadie was too stupid to take her pills regular, and don't want to say that to me."

"We got to have a serious talk," I say to Sadie that evening. We are sitting in the kitchen of One-wounds' cabin.

"I guess we do," she say, looking at the floor.

"I want to clear something up once and for all. You been around Etta and me long enough to know there is more than one way of telling the truth. When I asked if you forgot to take your pills, you said no. But that could also mean that you didn't forget, that you on purpose didn't take them. Is that what happened?"

Sadie raise her face from where she been studying the green-and-black tiles on the kitchen floor. And I don't need any more of an answer than the look in her eyes. She has never been able to lie.

She try real hard not to cry, but tears come anyway, roll silent out of her eyes and track down her cheeks.

"Why?" I say.

Sadie make a long sniffle. "If you really wanted a baby," I say, "you could of asked. We could have talked about it. "

"I was afraid I'd lose you," Sadie say real soft. "Lots of people read your books these days. You get to travel around. You been on the radio and the TV. I'm afraid you're gonna want a smart and pretty wife, maybe even a white one. I thought if we had a baby . . ."

Late that evening after I spent about four hours walking down the dirt roads of the reserve, thinking, I stop by Mad Etta's cabin and let her in on my troubles.

"If it was an accident I'd marry her in a minute, but I hate to feel I been trapped. I love Sadie a lot, but if I get married just to please her, I know I'm going to resent her for it."

"Two things," say Etta, "first, lots of couples live together and have babies without being married; and, second, it also possible to get rid of the baby. Sadie was dead wrong to do what she done, and I told her that when she was here a few days ago. My advice is to take a month to sort out the possibilities; you might come to like the idea of having a wife and baby."

I wonder how Etta knew?

Sadie and me always got along real good and her being pregnant don't change that a bit.

On a day when I get in the mail a small check for one of the stories I had printed up, me and Sadie drive up to Edmonton in Louis Coyote's pickup truck. Sadie sit close beside me, and though she is only four months along, I'm sure her belly is already pushing out the waist of her jeans.

"I can feel my breasts changing," she say to me, and smile. "I can feel them growing. Maybe they'll stay big after the baby comes." Sadie always been pretty small that way, not like Frank's girl Connie who burst out of her blouses.

"I got bigger boobs than Sadie," Frank has been known to say, and Sadie laugh along with us, but not very happily.

Being pregnant do agree with Sadie. "She is rounding off some of her corners," is the way Mad Etta put it. Sadie always been sharp-featured with no meat on her bones.

We have decided we will get married come the end of the summer. We will look for a small apartment in Wetaskiwin where the three of us can live while I finish up my terms at the Tech School. We also agree to let Frank plan the wedding, all but the bridge burning.

That afternoon we go shopping at the West Edmonton Mall, which is about a quarter-section of stores, also got a carnival and a skating rink all under one roof. We buy Sadie a red-and-white candy-striped maternity top, and she so pleased with it she wear it away from the store. She also pull me into a store for babies, and we pick out a dress of pink silky stuff, got about nine little petticoats under it. Sadie is positive she going to have a girl, and that would make me happy. Frank is the only one who really wants a boy.

"Anybody can make a girl," he says, "but it takes a real man to put a handle on the finished product."

That is one of the happiest days we ever spent together. I am getting excited about the baby too. We go to a movie and out for hamburgers, where we talk about naming our daughter. Sadie think it would be nice to name her Sigourney, after the movie star. I would rather give her an Indian name, something like Wolverine Woman. We decide maybe we will do both. We driving on the outskirts of the city, Sadie half asleep with her head on my shoulder, when she take sick.

The University Hospital in Edmonton was closest to where we were. By the time I get Sadie into emergency there already blood stains between the legs of her jeans.

They only keep her for one day, give her some shots to make sure any infection don't start.

"She'll be good as new in a week," the doctor say when I pick her up to take her home.

Maybe physically. But it been two months since that happened and Sadie still walk around like a dead person.

We'd made so many plans, and to have them snatched away from us was pretty hard to take. I know I feel, for most of a month, like I'm carrying a hundred pounds of lead inside me.

I do everything I can think of to make Sadie feel like her old self. I even suggest it would be alright if she wanted to get pregnant again. I say we'll get married just like we planned. But nothing help. The doctors say Sadie is healthy, give her some pills to make her feel better but they don't seem to help. We even make love, but only a couple times. There is nothing in the world worse than making love with someone who don't share your enthusiasm. Sadie just sit and stare at the little pink dress we bought that day; her hair get dull and matted, sometimes she don't even look up when someone calls her name. One night after she was asleep I took the little dress away and stuffed it in the Goodwill box at Wheatlands Shopping Center parking lot. But Sadie don't even ask what happened to it.

"*Depression?*" say Etta. "*Post natal depression?*"

I nod. "That's what the doctors say is wrong with Sadie."

"Doctors are too smart for their own good these days," say Etta. "They give people excuses. Your friend, Frank, have the right idea when he says, 'Life is hard and then you die.' We live. We die. There ain't much else. Best anybody can do is try to make living tolerable and dying painless."

"I came here hoping you might cheer me up," I say.

"Get me a beer from the bucket inside the door there," say Etta. She, as usual, sits way up on her tree trunk chair at the back of the cabin, where the light from the coal-oil lamp make her look like a copper colored goddess of some kind.

"Let me tell you a story, Silas. This happen to somebody I know well, oh, I bet, forty years ago. She was a young woman, married to a good man who loved her a lot. She was pregnant with their first baby. That husband was the happiest man on the reserve; he already made that baby a tiny drum, built him a medicine bag of his own, made a *tikenagan* (a carrying pouch) out of elk hide, tanned until it was soft as moss. The woman was seven months along when she took sick. The baby died inside her. The medicine man, Buffalo-who-walks-like-a-man, came to the *tipi*, used all the magic he had in his power, just to save the woman's life.

"That woman wasn't glad to be alive anymore. She grieved over that dead baby; she said over and over how she wished she'd died and the baby had lived, or that they both had died. Her husband was a gentle, patient man; but everyone, no matter how good a person, have a limit to their patience. He was a wise man and a believer in the old ways of the tribe. He went to the medicine man, Buffalo-who-walks like a-man; they spent a few hours in the sweat lodge together; they smoked a pipe, and sat silent across from each other in the medicine man's tent for most of a night.

"In the morning the husband said 'I think we should place my wife in the *tipi* of sorrow.'

"Buffalo-who-walks-like a-man nodded his head. 'I hoped that is what you would say. You have decided wisely.'

"In the real old days, grieving was a bitter process. Women cut off a finger joint when a relative died; both men and women scarred their arms in mourning; it was a custom for a grieving family to give away or to burn every one of their possessions.

"The husband, with the help of the medicine man, turned his own *tipi* into what was called a house of sorrow. He hauled out everything except the large bed, which was made by stuffing tanned hides with sweet clover. He gave away all his and his wife's possessions. She lay on the bed and stared at the smoke-hole, not caring what went on around her.

" 'This week is yours to grieve as you see fit,' the husband said. 'but it is to be the last week of your grief. Life goes on for us all.'

"The first morning the women of the tribe brought small gifts for the wife, a venison steak, a smoked quail breast, a dish of fresh-picked saskatoon berries. Most of them didn't speak, just pushed open the tent flap, smiled, and set the offering on the packed dirt floor.

"All week long the procession continued, children picked her bright bouquets of dandelions, fireweed, cowslips, or left her pretty stones they had found on the river bottom, left them shyly outside the tent. The woman all but ignored their efforts.

"Over the course of the week almost everyone in the tribe made a small gift to the woman. Many were pieces of clothing, a bowl, a household item; all things she would need to start her life over. One evening the women of the tribe gathered in front of the tent and sang a song encouraging her to join them in celebrating life.

"At the end of the week a celebration was planned. All week long when the women or children had been gathering firewood, they brought home an extra branch, or piece of deadfall. Now they all came slowly toward the tent of sorrow, moving stealthily, almost in slow motion, as if they were parting thick fog with each step, each carrying their burden of dry wood. The wood was stacked at the side of the tent.

"Buffalo-who-walks-like-a-man beat on his sacred drum. The men of the tribe, dressed in their finest beaded leather, their faces smeared with paint, drummed the day away. They, too, called for the woman to join them, to begin her life again.

"But the woman didn't come out. Inside the tent she lay like a log, her face buried in her bed. She knew what would happen if she didn't rejoin the tribe. She'd seen it once when she was a child.

"As darkness approached, the stack of firewood near the tent was lit. The drumming continued. The light from the fire reflected off the night sky and down through the smoke hole of the tent. It made patterns on the bed, like moonlight on water.

"The drumming got louder and the fire got brighter and higher. The old medicine man, Buffalo-who-walks-like-a-man, sit himself down cross-legged in front of the tent and sing to the woman, telling her how everybody is waiting for her come out and start her new life.

"When he don't get an answer he nod to the men who stoking the fire, one of them was the woman's husband, and they pile the new brush on the side of the fire run it right to the edge of the tent. Another minute and the fire will take the tent and the woman.

"The woman, who for all the weeks since she lost her baby felt she had nothing to live for, decide to take one last look at the sky before she die. She open her eyes and see the fire flickering off the sky and onto her own body and the shiny hair of the bear hide she was laying on. The inside of the tent get really hot; the fire started up the side of the tent, she could see it climbing the outside, like the sun do when it first rise in the morning.

"And with that she started thinking of the sun, and the striped tiger lilies that grew around the edges of the camp, and her husband who had been so gentle and patient with her these past months.

"Just as the fire burst through the wall of the tent, the flaps parted and the woman emerged. The rhythm of the drums changed from solemn to happy and the people began to dance. The woman's husband came to her and led her in among the dancers. Everyone came and hugged her and said how much they loved her and how glad they were she had chosen to live. They all celebrated far into the night, and the woman and her husband were given more bedding, clothing, utensils—all the things they needed to start a new life."

Etta stare down at me from her deep-set eyes, exhale to show the story finished, sound like a tractor tire deflating. I'm not sure what I'm supposed to have learned. That was then, this is now. Customs like that died out years ago.

"That woman was the medicine man's daughter," Etta say.

"You're a medicine man's daughter," I said.

"Yes, I am," said Etta with none of the sarcasm in her voice that I expected after my stupid statement.

Etta don't give me any advice or tell me any more stories. She just yawn and head over to her bed, make it plain it's time for me to go home.

I walk down to the Hobbema Pool Hall and tell Frank what just happen to me.

"No problem," says Frank. "A Fencepost understands these mysterious stories."

"What do *you* think I should do?"

"Improvise," says Frank. "We going to have to improvise. But that's something I'm good at. Remember how, when we were kids, I used to ride all the girls on the crossbar of my bicycle? Not one of them ever noticed it was a girl's bike . . . ."

"I think Sadie will get better by herself," I say.

But she don't. In fact she get worse. A lot worse. A couple of weeks later I take her to the doctor in Wetaskiwin and he put her in the hospital, where they don't do nothing for her but put her on a lot of medication make her move in slow motion.

After a week a doctor stop me in the hall as I leaving, "Mr. One-wound?" he say, assuming I am Sadie's husband. "We have a form at the desk for you to sign. We're going to try a different approach in treatment. It is a simple permission form for us to use electric shock therapy."

I tell him I got to check with the tribal medicine man before I can sign something like that.

"Bring it back tomorrow afternoon," he say, staring at me like I was a lot stranger than he expected me to be.

For one more time Etta surprise me.

"I'm glad to see they finally getting down to serious business," she say when I tell her of the shock treatments they want to do on Sadie.

"You're glad?"

"I suggested the same thing a month ago," she say, and look more smug than she usually do when people talk about medicine. "You wouldn't do anything then. How about now?"

"Native shock treatments?" I say.

"We had our treatment when doctors were still slitting wrists to let out bad blood. Like anything from primitive times, if it works it's a 100% cure, if it don't the loss is total."

"But Sadie doesn't know the story you told me. She won't understand what's happening."

"You'll tell her the basics. We'll get her off all the white man's medication, so her head will be clear. She's an Indian. She'll catch on."

"One of the Indian Affairs houses up on the ridge has been abandoned," I say. "We could use it; it going to be torn down anyway."

"You have to give away everything you *both* own. You'll have to part with your typewriter," Etta is saying. But I'm only half-listening. Visiting Sadie these past weeks, I seen the poor, stumbling, empty-eyed people who the doctors haven't been able to help, even with shock treatments. If I'm going to lose Sadie I'd rather lose her in a flash of fire, than see her exist in one of the dark wards of that brown-smelling hospital. I'm thinking too of Etta and maybe Rufus Firstrider sitting in front of the abandoned cabin drumming, and a whole lot of people standing around while the fire whooshes up into the night sky inching closer and closer to the cabin.

Also Available

The Fencepost Chronicles

Winner of the Stephen Leacock Award for Humour

In the fascinating universe of W.P. Kinsella there's no place quite like Hobbema, Alberta, where the Cree Indians of the Ermineskin Reserve live out their absurd, touching and hilarious adventures.

The Fencepost Chronicles contains thirteen wonderful stories featuring the delightfully zany Frank Fencepost and his friend Silas Ermineskin—as they cause a riot on a nude beach in Vancouver, chit-chat with the Queen in her bedroom and take their hockey team, the Hobbema Wagonburners, on the road. Throughout it all Frank and Silas remain undaunted, though not always unbloodied, as they and their fellow Cree pit themselves against travel agents, bureaucrats, used-car dealers and the RCMP.

"Kinsella defines a world in which magic and reality combine to make us laugh and think about the perceptions we take for granted." —*New York Times*

"These are wonderful stories, light-hearted, funny and fantastical." —*London Free Press*

Also Available

Brother Frank's Gospel Hour

"These are clever, entertaining stories, often tender, skillfully written. Silas, Frank and the others have become old and honored friends." —*The Edmonton Journal*

Silas Ermineskin and Frank Fencepost, last seen wrestling beauty queens and corrupt politicians in *The Miss Hobbema Pageant*, are back in the satirical and magical *Brother Frank's Gospel Hour*.

W.P. Kinsella returns to Hobbema, Alberta, for eleven new stories about the trials and tribulations of Silas Ermineskin and his friends and relations. Included in the cast of zany characters are Mad Etta, who searches for the giant saskatoon berries that will make her bannock famous, Jason Twelve Trees, who fights to become the first boy to participate in the Wetaskiwin Recreation Commission Cooking Competition, and, of course, Frank Fencepost, who hits a gold mine when he decides to try his hand at evangelism on Hobbema's new radio station.

"You just can't help but cheer for these lovable rogues as they con and odd-job their way through Western Canada... This may well be Kinsella's best to date." —*Star Phoenix (Saskatoon)*

"...a collection of gems..." —*The Calgary Sun*